"Martin Suter has found a new tone in the detective novel: a blend of reserve and attention to detail with clock-work precision ... Suter is as charming as his hero when he uses the conventions of the genre."

—LE MONDE

"One couldn't imagine anything more diverting than a second novel with this team in the lead roles."

—DER SPIEGEL

"Masterful."

—WESTFÄLISCHE NACHRICHTEN

ALLMEN

AND THE

DRAGONFLIES

MARTIN SUTER

Translated by Steph Morris

NEW VESSEL PRESS

NEW YORK

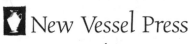

www.newvesselpress.com

First published in German in 2011 as *Allmen und die Libellen*
Copyright © 2011 Diogenes Verlag AG Zürich
Translation Copyright © 2018 Stephen Morris

Dragonfly image by E. A. Séguy,
from *E. A. Séguy's Insectes* (QL466 .S49 1920), Plate 10,
Special Collections Research Center at NCSU Libraries.

Library of Congress Cataloging-in-Publication Data
Suter, Martin
[Allmen und die Libellen. English]
Allmen and the Dragonflies/ Martin Suter; translation by Steph Morris.
p. cm.
ISBN 978-1-939931-57-3
Library of Congress Control Number 2017910568
I. Switzerland — Fiction

For Toni

ALLMEN

AND THE

DRAGONFLIES

PART I

1

The gray light made everything flat and lifeless. Dawn was on pause.

It was chilly in Allmen's glasshouse library. Perhaps he should light a fire. But the previous attempt, last winter, had failed so miserably that he dropped the idea. He sat in his reading chair, without a book, and shivered. It didn't matter.

The legs of his grand piano had left three deep imprints in the floor. Even this sight left him unmoved. Nothing but crushing indifference.

He had no idea how much time had passed since he'd seen Carlos approaching the house in his coat and woolly hat. He'd heard him rush up the stairs then come down shortly after. Carlos had not come by the room. Having seen no light, he would have assumed Allmen was in the Viennois. Like every morning at this time.

Now he saw Carlos was busy outside. He was wearing his work clothes, an older woolly hat, and a work jacket with a thick lining.

Allmen would just sit here and wait till he came in to make lunch. He would go into the kitchen and say, "Carlos?"

And Carlos would reply, *"Qué manda?"*

And then he would say, "The time has come. I need *las libélulas.*"

And if he handed them over, Allmen would put the plan into action. And if not? That didn't matter either.

He must have dozed off. But finally he heard sounds from the kitchen. It had gotten darker. It would start snowing at any moment.

Allmen eased himself out of the armchair. As he passed the spot where the rear of the greenhouse faced a tall thicket of trees, he sensed something move there.

The trees grew dense and dark there, the stems of tall pines and spruce rising through an impenetrable undergrowth of yew and bracken. Sometimes Allmen saw an urban fox emerge or vanish at this spot, searching for something to eat in the gardens and forecourts of the villa district.

He stepped back, stood in front of the glass panel and stared at the undergrowth.

He felt a hard blow to his chest. As he fell, he heard a muffled thud, and sensed pain at the back of his head.

2

Half past ten in the morning was a nice time to be in Café Viennois, perhaps the nicest.

The dregs of the previous night were gone, and the staleness of the day had not yet set in. It smelled of the hissing Lavazza at which Gianfranco was now frothing the milk for a cappuccino, of the croissants on the bar and on the tables, of perfumes and *eaux de toilettes* from the handful of idlers and flâneurs to whom the Viennois belonged at this time.

One of them was reading a book, an English paperback with the spine broken so he could read it with one hand like an airport novel, the other hand free for his late breakfast and the cold cigarette butt he had held for years to help him quit smoking.

Over the arm of his two-seater plush wingback lay a beige raincoat. The man wore a mouse-gray suit, sitting well on him even as he slouched, a thin, fine-patterned tie, and an eggshell shirt with a soft, narrow collar. He was probably a little over forty. His nicely chiseled face did not deserve such a flat nose.

On the white tablecloth was a solid china saucer, empty except for the remains of a croissant, and a large cup, almost empty, coated inside with milk froth. The man was one of the last guests at the Viennois to order "a bowl," as a café au lait was once known.

Gianfranco brought over a fresh cup on an oval chrome tray, and removed the empty. "Signor Conte," he murmured.

"Grazie," Allmen replied, without looking up.

His full name was von Allmen, with the stress on von. It was a very common family name, one thousand, seven hundred and thirty eight of them in the phone book, and despite the aristocratic heritage implied by the preposition "von," the name "von Allmen" originally meant nothing more than "from the Alps." As a young man, however, Allmen began to omit the "von" in a spirit of republicanism, lending it a significance it never had.

He did the opposite with his two forenames, Hans and Fritz, taken from his two grandfathers according to the family tradition. He soon cleansed them of their bucolic stench, going to some bureaucratic effort to ennoble them to Johann and Friedrich. His friends called him John, and he introduced himself to new people simply and modestly as Allmen. But on official documents he was called Johann Friedrich von Allmen. And the envelopes he fetched from his post office box on the way to a late breakfast at the Viennois and then placed carelessly next to his coffee cup, were addressed to a Herr Johann Friedrich v. Allmen, as was written on his personalized stationery. This abbreviation not only saved space, it automatically shifted the stress from the "o" of von onto the "A" of Allmen. It had also elevated him to the title of "Conte," which Gianfranco had bestowed on him, only half in jest.

Most of the post-ten o'clock guests at the Viennois knew one another. However they still adhered strictly to the unwritten seating plan, some of them alone at their tables, a variety of jackets, bags, briefcases and reading material distributed around them so no one would consider joining them, others in pairs, always with the same partner, and others in small groups, also identical each day. Some of the post-ten guests greeted one another audibly, some nodded in silence, some had ignored one another for years.

One of the regular groups was seated two tables away from Allmen. Four shop owners, all around sixty, met there every day except Sunday from a quarter past ten to a quarter to eleven. Theirs and Allmen's times thus overlapped by fifteen minutes.

One of the four knew Allmen a little better. He owned an upmarket antiques business nearby. His name was Jack Tanner, an elegant man in his late fifties, who sauntered through his antiques as if they were there not to be sold but solely to satisfy his aesthetic demands. He justified the exorbitant prices of his wares simply due to his appearance. He exercised the discretion crucial to the trade, toward those buying and also those selling. This had encouraged Allmen to choose Tanner when forced occasionally to sell one of the more choice items in his collection. Neither gave the slightest indication, during their fleeting encounters at the Viennois, that they also had professional dealings.

Outside the window next to Allmen's table, the passersby began putting up their umbrellas. The gray soup which had hung over the roofs was now drizzling down on the city, like cold, wet dust. Allmen put off leaving and ordered another cup of coffee.

It was shortly after eleven thirty when he got ready to leave, although the weather had still not improved. He gave Gianfranco the signal for the check, signed it, and pressed a ten franc note into the waiter's hand. Allmen had learned to invest the little money he had in his creditworthiness, not in subsistence.

Gianfranco brought his coat, accompanied Allmen to the door and, lost in thought, watched the figure in the raincoat, collar turned up, as he disappeared between the umbrellas, murmuring, *"Un cavaliere."*

3

The Intercity, with tilt technology, shot through the mist-shrouded vineyards around Lake Neuchâtel, of which not even the shores were visible. Allmen had a compartment to himself. On the blue seat next to him lay a capacious pilot's case in brown pigskin. He continued to read his thriller.

As the gentle microphone voice announced Yverdon-les-Bains, he broke off reading. The name awoke memories from his childhood. He had often heard it at the dinner table in the early eighties. His father had invested a lot of money in agricultural land in the area, hoping that when that section of the A5 highway was finished it would be rezoned for construction. The strategy failed, and instead of blaming his poor French, Allmen's father put it down to the "Gallic incompetence" of the Yverdon local politicians.

This was one of his father's few business errors. He had left Allmen a fortune of millions. Its foundation was a single land-use decision in which, as people noted in the village at the time, he was not uninvolved. The Schwarzacker, the largest field on his farm, was incorporated into a construction zone. And thanks to the opening of a new highway section, it was soon part of the city's commuter belt. Which boosted the real estate value considerably. Allmen's father acquired a taste for this process and began systematically investing in agricultural land in potential commuter belts. The strategy paid off frequently enough that after his untimely death—regularly and generously entertaining local politicians with influence over land-use decisions took its toll—he was able to leave his only son enough money to ensure that if he was prudent and economical, he would never have to work again.

Prudence and economy were among the few qualities which Fritz, as his father still called him after he changed his name, lacked. He was not a numbers person. His field was languages. He found them easy and enjoyable to learn, and for years had spent his time studying them in the capital cities of this world. Alongside Swiss German, his first language, he spoke fluent, accent-free French, Italian, English, Portuguese and Spanish. He could converse in Russian and Swedish, and could produce flawless broadcaster's German if needed, but had discovered that his Swiss accent made a better impression.

And so he led the life of a carefree international student till his father's trustees informed him of his sudden death.

Kurt Fritz von Allmen was only sixty-two and had assumed he still had plenty of time to put his affairs in order. A widower, he had not made a will. His current partner received nothing, and although he was aware of his sole heir's extravagant lifestyle, he had not left any instructions for managing his wealth.

During his life he had kept Fritz on a long leash. He had trained in agriculture and had no idea what the maintenance costs of an international student might be. He was also proud of his educated son and proud that he could enable him to have it better than he had. Allmen's father had not travelled much. Earlier, as a farmer, the cows had kept him at home. Later it was business. He had no idea what hotels in Paris and New York cost, what you had to pay for shoes and clothes in London, and how great the price difference between economy and first class was. If Allmen's father lacked urbaneness, his son had too much of it.

Allmen returned to his book. Morges had just been announced.

4

Allmen put on his most affected British accent as he informed the shopkeeper he wished only to look around. The woman was around fifty and had emerged from the back room as soon as Allmen entered. She switched straight to English. If he had any questions, he shouldn't hesitate to ask.

The antiques shop was lined with shelves and vitrines. It specialized in china, selling everything from cheap bric-a-brac to costly Meissen statuettes and priceless Chinese vases and figurines.

Allmen took his time, went from object to object, pausing at the pieces which seized his attention, examining them, leaning forward, as closely as he could without using his hands.

He skimmed over a square vase labeled *"Période Kangxi, famille verte, CHF 8300"* and focused on four bright yellow teacups. Both cups and saucers were edged in gold, and each cup bore the emblem of the Hamburg America Line. The set was priced at three hundred francs.

"I'll take these," he said to the shopkeeper in smug Oxford English. She had been following him at a discreet distance throughout his tour. "Would you mind wrapping them individually as a present, if it's not too much trouble."

And then she did what he had hoped she would. She carried the cups and saucers, two at a time, into the back room.

As soon as he heard her busy with paper and scissors, he checked once again that there wasn't a security camera lurking anywhere, went to the shelf with the Kangxi vase, and slid it into the large inside pocket of his overcoat.

Then he stood at the door to the back room and chatted with the shopkeeper while she finished gift-wrapping the cups.

"For my wife," he explained. "Today is our anniversary. I do hope the plane to London isn't canceled with all this fog."

5

When Jack Tanner entered the Viennois the next morning, Allmen was already there, and gave him a nod, pointing discreetly to the pilot's case on the chair next to him. Tanner nodded back. An hour later Allmen was standing outside his shop.

It was among the last unrenovated buildings in the center of the banking district. It had already been an antiques shop when Tanner took it over nearly thirty years ago. He had adopted the name, *Les Trouvailles*, from his predecessor. Not because he particularly liked it, but because the old-fashioned sign had appealed to him, with polished brass letters against a dark green panel.

The shop had three modest windows made of security glass, with old-fashioned sensors which would sound an alarm in the case of burglary. Or perhaps not. The system had never been put to the test.

One of the other security measures at *Les Trouvailles* was that the door was always locked. Customers had to ring the bell, which Allmen now did.

After a while Jack Tanner came to the door in person. Since his longtime assistant Frau Freitag had retired, he ran the business alone. There was little passing trade, and most customers wanted to talk directly with the proprietor. When he was with his breakfast club at the Viennois the "Back Soon" sign hung on the door.

The display and sales area of the shop was walled with built-in vitrines, part of the original fittings. The objects within were lit with adjustable spotlights attached to an electrified track on the ceiling. In the middle stood a range of tabletop vitrines for jewelry, silver and smaller china pieces. The room exuded a dusty elegance and smelled of the wax used to polish the creaking parquet floor.

A sliding door led to a side room, half of which was used to display furniture, the other half as a storeroom. From there a door led to Tanner's tiny office, the sacristy as he called it. Allmen followed him in. The room was dominated by a Biedermeier desk with an upholstered swiveling chair from the same period. Both had stood in General Guisan's office at his World War Two command center, Tanner claimed, so were not for sale. For visitors there was just a two-seater, Louis Philippe sofa.

Tanner did not invite Allmen to sit on it. He pointed to his desk and said, "Show me what you've got."

The discreet commercial relationship between the two went back years. At the beginning Allmen had been a good customer, mainly buying American silver and Art Deco. Later, when Allmen's financial difficulties forced him to act, he turned from customer to supplier. He regularly sold Tanner items from his collection. Tanner was stingy, but what he lacked in generosity, he made up for in discretion.

Over the years Allmen's stock of superfluous pieces had shrunk so low he began to search flea markets and provincial shops for saleable items. The prices Jack offered left Allmen with such narrow margins, he was forced to look for another solution. He found it by chance in an antiques shop in Alsace. He was buying a small statue of the Madonna, and while the shop assistant was busy packing it up, he thought: I could swipe that set of Rosenthal figures if I wanted. No one would notice. And he found he did want to.

Over time he perfected the technique of distracting the sales staff with a purchase so he could liberate something unnoticed. His clothes, his manner, and the fact he was buying something, made him seem trustworthy, remembered as someone above suspicion.

Although he parted with money readily, Allmen guarded his modest working capital fiercely. It financed his decoy purchases and the train journeys. He worked strictly at a certain distance from the city where he lived.

Allmen unpacked the vase and placed it on the desk.

Jack Tanner picked it up, examined it, and said, "two thousand."

Tanner's offers were always final. Only very rarely did he provoke Allmen to put up a little resistance. Allmen knew it would earn him nothing but a shrug.

He had no option but to accept Tanner's offers. He was his only buyer. He must have realized that Allmen's goods were no longer coming from his own collection. But he never asked about their provenance. And Allmen had never seen one of his items in the storeroom or display area of *Les Trouvailles*.

Tanner must have had customers he could call who were equally discreet and did not ask questions about provenance.

Allmen nodded, took the money and said goodbye. Till next time.

6

The cast-iron gate to his house had been freshly painted. Glossy black, with gold for the finials on top of the gateposts, which continued along the railings either side of the gate next to the box hedge. Allmen thought it looked a little nouveau riche, but better than the rust it replaced.

On the right-hand pillar were two brass signs, one smaller, one larger. On the larger was written "K. C. L. & D. Trust" and on the smaller "J. F. V. A."

On the left-hand pillar was an intercom, also made of polished brass, with two buttons. The upper was labeled "K. C. L. & D." and the lower "J. F. V. A."

Allmen pressed the lower one.

After a few seconds a suspicious male voice asked, "Yes?"

"*Soy yo,*" Allmen replied. "It's me."

The lock buzzed and Allmen stepped onto the paved path leading to the carved oak door of the villa. About halfway along it he disappeared behind an impeccably manicured box.

He had turned down one of the pathways leading around the villa through its grounds.

A well-kept lawn, here and there ericaceous beds for rhododendrons and azaleas, already displaying their fall color. All of it guarded by imposing ranks of mature trees: grand firs, cedars, maples and magnolias.

There, in the permanent shade of the trees, stood a small gardener's cottage, with a greenhouse attached to its western façade.

The door was open, and in the tiny vestibule Allmen was met by a man. He had smooth, neatly parted blue-black hair, and the features of a Maya. He was wearing a white waiter's jacket with a white shirt, black pants and a black tie. Allmen greeted him in Spanish.

"Hola Carlos."

"Muy buenas tardes, Don John," Carlos replied, took his wet raincoat, hung it on a hanger and walked with it to a door under the steep wooden steps which led to the attic. Their threshold was two steps lower than the hallway floor.

Behind this was a room that had previously functioned as the laundry for the villa, suitably ample for this role. Now there was just one washing machine and a dryer, with a couple of clothes lines. The majority of the room was filled with boxes and furniture, from floor to ceiling. It was here that Allmen stored the items from his former life that were either indispensable or unsellable.

Carlos hung the raincoat on one of the washing lines and returned to the tiny vestibule. Allmen was standing there in front of the console, above which hung a gilded cloakroom mirror. A letter was lying there, which was unusual, because letters to him were usually addressed to his post office box. He preferred his creditors not to know where he lived.

He tucked it away in his pocket. He would read it later.

The flavors of the lunch Carlos was keeping on a low flame wafted through the open kitchen door. Allmen knew the smell: Carlos's homesickness food. Black beans—*frijoles*. They would be accompanied by guacamole flavored with chili, lemon and fresh coriander, fried mince patties—*tortitas de carne*—and maize pancakes—*tortillas*.

It was not Allmen's favorite food, but he couldn't complain. He hadn't given Carlos any housekeeping money for ages.

They entered the only room that came close to meeting Allmen's standards, the library. It had twice the floor space of the gardener's cottage. Along its walls stood enormous bookcases that on closer inspection had clearly been built to fit a different room. The room was very light considering the weather and its shady location. It was walled in glass. This was the property's former greenhouse.

Its concrete floor was almost entirely covered with carpets. There was a suite of Art Deco chairs, a lectern, a writing desk, a cast-iron wood burner with two comfortable worn-leather armchairs and a set of mahogany library steps on wheels. There were two standard lamps for reading at night, and a slightly battered candelabra to provide a more festive atmosphere.

On the far side of the greenhouse was a black Bechstein baby grand. Allmen was a talented if slapdash pianist who often used to play bar music to entertain his guests. He still improvised on his own sometimes, to relax.

Allmen sat in one of the leather armchairs and took out the letter. Carlos placed a side table within reach and put the sherry on it.

The envelope was embossed with the crest of the Kingdom of Morocco and the letterhead of its Consulate General. It was addressed with a fountain pen. Allmen ripped it open and took out the letter.

The same fountain pen had been used to write: "12,455 Swiss francs including interest. Final deadline Wednesday!! Or else …!!!"

Signed: "H. Dörig."

Allmen felt his chest tense, as it did when long suppressed unpleasantness suddenly reared up. He swapped the letter for the sherry on the side table and took a swig. As a matter of principle, Allmen never opened letters he suspected might contain anything unpleasant. This way he maintained the calm necessary in his situation.

He wouldn't have credited the coarse Dörig with the Moroccan-Consulate-General trick. How had he got hold of the stationery?

Allmen took another swig of sherry and attempted to suppress all thought of Dörig. The man was his most unpleasant creditor. He was aggressive, perhaps even violent. An antiques dealer from Oberland, he had barns full of stock, which he sold to retailers, much of it without receipts. Allmen knew him from the old days. In and among Dörig's jumble of rough-hewn farmhouse furniture, dusty horse tackle and woodworm-ridden spinning wheels, he would often discover superb collector's items. In his time as a collector Allmen had been a regular there. And very popular, as he had sometimes paid more than Dörig asked. Not because he liked him, but he didn't want to be taken for a bargain hunter. Allmen despised bargains. They were beneath his dignity and should be beneath everyone's dignity. Things should cost whatever they were worth, otherwise it was all too sordid.

Thanks to this attitude, Dörig had let him buy things on credit. Allmen had been making ends meet for some time by selling individual pieces from his collection. Once it had shrunk to the indispensible—from both a practical and sentimental perspective—he had begun to buy objects cheaply and sell them on at a profit. By then he could no longer afford to despise bargains. In his situation, Allmen could not be choosy. One of his suppliers was Dörig, and he had built up quite a debt with him. Dörig had warned him twice verbally, and after Allmen ceased to visit him, had probably warned him in writing a few times. Now he had resorted to threatening letters.

Allmen emptied his glass, leaned his head back and gazed at the ceiling. The drizzle had risen to a persistent downpour, streaming down the glass roof in a restless film.

At the corner of one of the glass panes the mortise joint was leaking. He would inform Carlos, who would mark the spot on the floor with tape and later plug the leaking joint with putty. One of Carlos's many duties.

Now he called him for lunch. Carlos insisted on punctuality, as he had to return to his paid job as gardener and caretaker at two o'clock on the dot.

Throughout the meal he waited on Allmen, although Allmen had asked him countless times to sit down with him to eat. Carlos insisted on eating in the kitchen.

Once he had cleared the table and piled the dishes in the kitchen sink, Allmen heard him climbing the stairs. A few minutes later he returned wearing his gardening outfit and a rain cape and asked, *"Algo más, Don John?"*

"No, gracias, Carlos," Allmen answered.

Carlos wished him an enjoyable afternoon, went back into the library and marked the wet spot on the floor, which Allmen had already forgotten.

7

———

Allmen habitually rested for half an hour in the afternoon. This little siesta didn't just refresh him, it also reminded him every day that he was privileged to be a man of independent means. Even after all these years, sleeping while the rest of the country was pursuing productive activity gave him a sense of enormous happiness he knew only from cutting class at school. He called it "cutting life."

There was nothing more delicious than closing the curtains on whatever was going on outside, slipping under the cool quilt in your underwear and listening to the distant sounds of the world with half-closed eyes. Only to emerge from your afternoon snooze shortly afterward, amazed and invigorated.

His bedroom was filled by a king-size bed, a bookshelf for his nighttime reading matter and two closets for the section of his wardrobe appropriate to the time of year. The rest of his clothes were also stored in the laundry.

He lay in bed, next to him a paperback for the unlikely situation he was unable to doze off. The rain pattered softly against the window, otherwise the world outside kept quiet.

He couldn't entirely banish Dörig's letter from his consciousness. Not because of the twelve thousand, four hundred and fifty five francs. He would find them somehow. It was the nature of this final demand which was disturbing him.

However badly Allmen managed money, he was extremely good at managing debt. He had learned that during his time at Charterhouse, the exclusive boarding school in Surrey where his father had sent him at fourteen at his own request. Allmen wanted to be cleansed of his family's nouveau riche, farmyard whiff, as he put it.

At Charterhouse handling debt was an unofficial part of the boys' education. Debt was nothing to be ashamed of. On the contrary, it was good for one's reputation to have some. For pedagogic reasons the school rules set a limit on the amount of pocket money pupils could be given. This led to a proliferation of money lending. Everyone boasted about their debts, looked up to those with the highest, deferred them or serviced them in installments, always paying them off with style and nonchalance.

Allmen had continued this in later life. Right from the start, the income from his inheritance had failed to match his growing need for capital, and his deceased father's trustees soon lost their patience. They were succeeded by a series of handpicked advisors, whose advice contributed more to Allmen's expenses than his income. He soon found himself forced to finance his lifestyle and his new acquisitions—alongside the Villa Schwarzacker these included apartments in Paris, London, New York, Rome and Barcelona—by parting with some of the more secure, solid assets his father had bequeathed him. And when he had used up that supply, he maintained himself via sales—mostly rash—of his new acquisitions, first the real estate, then furniture, then collector's items, then one by one the decreasing number of items which in his former life he had considered indispensible. And finally items acquired in a similar manner to the Kangxi vase.

As a rich man, Allmen had been a highly generous creditor. And now in his role as debtor, he expected the same patience and understanding from his creditors. Initially he was not disappointed. His former solvency stood him in good stead. What he had were not debts; they were outstanding payments, accounts, pending items. Creditor and debtor treated each other with the respect everyone owes someone they are dependent on.

And this was why Dörig's letter had opened up a new dimension. It was a crude, vulgar fit of rage from a man prepared to use violence, a category he had not yet encountered. Allmen abhorred all forms of violence. Including the verbal form.

He was seriously perturbed. But when he woke half an hour later from his siesta, amazed and refreshed as ever, this perturbation had receded into something quiet and distant.

8

The original owners of the Villa Schwarzacker, then called the Villa Odeon, had used the greenhouse to grow flowers, vegetables and fruit, and over winter potted palms and other nonhardy ornamentals. The owner previous to Allmen had neglected the greenhouse, using it as a shed and storeroom. But when Allmen took over the villa he had it restored because he bred orchids. Or rather, he had orchids bred.

He had acquired the taste while staying at a friend's colonial villa in Guatemala. They stood on every table, commode and sideboard, in every niche and on every ledge, always fresh, often smelling enchanting—no, it wasn't true that orchids had no fragrance—in every color and size.

It turned out that Carlos the gardener was also the orchid man of the house. He nursed and propagated them, brought them into the villa when they were in flower then back to the greenhouse afterward.

When Carlos first saw the greenhouse at Villa Schwarzacker, he said, in his formal manner, "Simply an idea, Don John, nothing more." And so the Villa Schwarzacker became famous during Allmen's time for the orchids which decorated it.

He had to give up the collection along with the villa. But Allmen was still reaping the benefits of restoring the greenhouse, above all the installation of modern gas heating. It ensured that this large, poorly insulated space was still inhabitable even in winter. The wood-burning stove Allmen now sat in front of was a luxury. And luxury was one of Allmen's greatest weaknesses.

He was proud of the deal he'd done on the gardener's cottage. When he was finally forced to sell the Villa Schwarzacker—he had renamed it in honor of the land which formed the cornerstone of the fortune he had inherited—he had the idea to sell only on the condition he was given the lifelong right to dwell in the cottage. Several of the buyers agreed, but he finally sold to the trust company because he liked the idea of having the place to himself evenings and weekends. And because the director agreed to let him have most of the bookshelves from the library. The director was pleased to have the extra wall space for the exhibitions the company put up during marketing events targeting current and potential clients.

Allmen had nearly finished the paperback, a new thriller by the great Elmore Leonard, now mellowed with age. The story consisted almost entirely of dialogue, with none of the violent scenes of his earlier work.

Allmen was addicted to reading. He had been even as a child. He had soon learned that reading was the simplest, most effective and nicest way of escaping what was going on around you. His father, who Allmen had never once seen holding a book, had the greatest respect for this passion of his son's. He always accepted reading as an excuse for his boy's many derelictions of duty. And his mother, that gentle, sickly woman, who died too young, leaving Allmen with only vague memories, accepted any excuses her husband accepted.

Even today Allmen read anything he could lay his hands on, world literature, the classics, the latest titles, biographies, brochures, instruction manuals ... He was a regular in several secondhand bookshops and had been known to hail a taxi when he saw books in a trash heap so he could take them home.

Allmen had to finish a book once he had started it, even if it was terrible. He did this not out of respect for the author, but out of curiosity. He believed that every book held a secret, even if it was only the answer to the question of why it had been written. He had to discover this secret. So really it was not reading Allmen was addicted to. He was addicted to secrets.

This trait had not just made him a bookworm. It was also responsible for his addiction to gossip. This addiction was passive, however. He loved hearing gossip, but it would never have occurred to him to spread it. Allmen was that paradoxical thing: a discreet gossip.

Out of one of the many small loudspeakers mounted on the bookshelves came Puccini's *La Bohème* in a recording featuring Callas and Di Stefano. A state-of-the-art hi-fi was on Allmen's list of basic needs—a list from which he had recently been forced to delete ever more items. He didn't think a bankruptcy auditor would see it that way, but things wouldn't get that bad, he was determined of that.

Allmen had left gaps of a few feet between some of the bookshelves so that some light entered from the sides and the view of the lovely garden wasn't completely blocked. These gaps could be filled by drawing the drapes, which was what he now did. The afternoon had become even more unappealing; a wind had risen, tearing leaves from the plane trees and driving the rain against the glass façade. If the weather didn't improve he would ask Carlos to light the stove tomorrow.

In a rare moment of self-sufficiency, he went into the kitchen and made himself a cup of tea all by himself.

9

The opera premiere subscription was another core item on Allmen's list of basic needs. If you couldn't afford that, you really were broke.

Allmen had already secured two of the most sought-after seats while his father was alive: center orchestra, fifth row. His father had made no objection to paying over four thousand francs each year because this counted as an investment in his son's education. He once accompanied his son to a *Magic Flute* premiere, but had to abandon his seat soon after the overture due to a persistent fit of coughing.

These days the two seats cost twice as much. They were still in the name of Johann Friedrich v. Allmen. However this season Allmen had sublet the second. One of his many wider acquaintances, Serge Lauber, an investment banker, had offered him six thousand francs, cash in hand. That was an offer Allmen could hardly refuse in his situation, as it financed half of his own seat too, and he had been behind with the subscription payments since the start of the season, although he hadn't received a reminder. With such long-standing subscribers and generous former donors one showed a little patience.

This wet fall evening it was the premiere of Puccini's *Madame Butterfly*. Allmen looked forward to the opera nights, which he always began with an aperitif in the Golden Bar and rounded off with a late supper from the small menu at Promenade.

He was wearing a midnight-blue tie, minimally patterned, and a seasonally dark suit made by his long neglected English tailor, under a navy cashmere overcoat made by the latter's equally neglected colleague in Rome.

Herr Arnold took his umbrella from him by way of a greeting and opened the door of his 1978 Fleetwood Cadillac. Allmen was a regular customer of Herr Arnold, who owned two taxis, a Mercedes diesel and this shiny black and chrome American conveyance, which he took out of the garage for fans, such as Allmen. For these customers Herr Arnold worked on account, sending a monthly invoice. The fact that these had been paid rather irregularly of late must surely be for administrative reasons. Someone who lived like that could hardly have money worries.

Allmen reclined on the wine red leather seat in the back of the Fleetwood, enjoying the short journey from the villa district to the city center. Herr Arnold, a compact, circumspect man in his sixties, was the kind of taxi driver who talked only when he was asked a question. He did not inflict his political, religious or traffic-related problems on his passengers. Allmen appreciated that nearly as much as the lovingly maintained interior of this whispering giant.

They glided slowly over the wet asphalt, lit by brake lights, headlights and streetlamps. The silhouettes of pedestrians and their umbrellas rushed past the shop windows. The loudest sound inside the car was the brief hiccup as one of the rubber seals on the windshield wipers caught every other time it returned down.

"Can you still get those seals?" Allmen asked, so that the journey wasn't quite so silent.

"No. I have to cut them to size myself. And if the rubber's too hard, or the strip's too narrow, this is what happens. Does it bother you?"

"Not in the slightest," Allmen said.

"Well it sure bothers me. It drives me crazy!" Herr Arnold fell silent, shocked at having revealed his innermost feelings.

Allmen assured him once more that he, the passenger, really wasn't disturbed by it. He had asked purely out of interest.

Shortly afterward, the car pulled up at the Golden Bar. Allmen signed the receipt for the journey and gave an ample tip to Herr Arnold, who then held up his umbrella for Allmen, accompanying him the few steps over the sidewalk to the entrance.

10

As its name implied, the Golden Bar was decorated, in the 1960s, with a great deal of gold. The shelves holding the bottles rested on gold bars, the counter and bar stools were gold painted, the mirrors and pictures gold framed, the ashtrays and snack dishes golden and the walls and ceiling papered with gold foil. Smoke and time had matted and darkened this excess of gold, leaving the bar looking more distinguished now.

Allmen was a habitué. The bartender, an aging Spaniard with over forty years bartending experience around the world, and a gallery of similarly darkened brass plaques from international cocktail mixing competitions, had already begun measuring tequila, Cointreau and lemon juice in a battered shaker full of ice cubes as soon as Allmen appeared.

Before the opera he always drank two margaritas. They put him in an expectant, cheerful and receptive mood. He sat on a bar stool and nodded to the bartender, who nodded back with a smile, wound a napkin around the shaker to protect his hands from the cold and began to shake—in his unfathomable rhythm, half the secret of his legendary cocktails.

The bar was full, the after-work crowd in business dress giving way to the first of the premiere crowd, of whom Allmen knew several faces, and nodded to them. His premiere subtenant, Serge Lauber, was nowhere to be seen. They normally met here and walked over to the opera house together. But sometimes he was delayed and they met in their seats.

The long-serving bar pianist was playing "Where or When," as always when Allmen was in the Golden Bar. And as always Allmen sent him a glass of house white, which the old man raised for a conspiratorial toast toward Allmen, without interrupting the music.

The bartender brought a fresh bowl of warm almonds and a second margarita. Allmen kept his eye on the door. The people arriving now were out of breath, their umbrellas dripping wet. Allmen was annoyed he hadn't asked Herr Arnold to wait, as he used to. Damned economizing!

He had already signed the check and left the bartender's tip on the gold tray when a woman entered the bar. She was wearing a calf-length, green mink coat, with a platinum blonde bob, cherry red lips and black sunglasses, which she raised now in the dim lighting, to look around the bar.

"You must be John," she said, holding out her hand. "I'm Joëlle. Most people call me Jojo."

Allmen slid off his bar stool and took the strong, green-gloved hand in his. He was certain he had never seen her before.

"Come on, it's time we left," Joëlle said.

Allmen must have stared at her in consternation, because now she burst out laughing. "Sorry, Serge gave me his ticket. He can't make it today."

Allmen fetched his coat and followed the woman. Outside the bar she was met by a young man with an umbrella. He accompanied first her and then him through the rain, now descending in bucketsful, to a Mercedes limousine parked half over the sidewalk with its hazard lights flashing.

During the short drive to the opera house Joëlle drank a whisky on the rocks from the icebox recessed into the backrest and smoked a cigarette. Allmen declined both offers. There was also time for her to tell him she lived in New York, but was staying with her father at the moment. He was pampering her after a ghastly divorce.

11

When Allmen came to help his new companion out of her coat at the coat check, she turned out to be wearing a kind of kimono, in honor of *Madame Butterfly*.

"Oh, a kimono," he said without thinking, and scoured the floor for a hole to sink into.

"Goes with the opera," Joëlle beamed and gave a little pirouette. Allmen was saved by the bell.

She must have been in her late thirties, not an especially beautiful woman, but she knew how to get around that. The strands of her bangs, backcombed at her hairline and reaching down to the bridge of her nose, hid her low forehead. Her small, close-set but wonderfully emerald eyes were enlarged with flamboyant use of eyeliner. She had an attractive, boyish figure, and made her way, even through the premiere throng, rushing toward their seats, with a dancer's grace.

During the overture her hand crept onto Allmen's thigh. By the end of the first act it had reached his crotch.

12

Jojo was snoring. She lay on her back in her larger-than-life bed, as the less-than-ladylike sound emerged from her less-than-cherry-red lips.

The sound wasn't wholly inappropriate, Allmen thought. That evening she had proved herself unladylike in every sense. Never in his life—and his life had been eventful in this regard—had a woman thrown herself on him with such insatiable hunger as this platinum-blonde opera acquaintance. In the back of the limousine, watched in the rearview mirror by the chauffeur's eyes, he had managed to fend off Jojo's advances. But once they were in the hall of the huge lakeside villa, he let her drag him up the wide flight of stairs and into her diva's bedroom like a lioness her prey.

There she undressed both of them simultaneously, threw herself onto the bed along with him, gobbled him up and then gave herself to him with a wantonness he had never encountered before.

Immediately afterward she had fallen into a deep sleep, and soon began to snore.

Allmen lay propped on his right arm and looked at her. The light was softened by the pink lampshade, but he could still see the marks of a life filled with too much sun, not enough sleep, too much fun and not enough love. He felt what he always felt in these situations: the connection he had persuaded himself he felt, without which he couldn't go to bed with a woman, had gone. He studied the stranger next to him without affection. This time it was worse: he felt used by her, and resented her for it.

He got up to look for a toilet.

13

The bedroom had two doors. They had entered via one of them, so the other must lead to the bath. He opened it, and found the light switch.

He was standing in a large, black-marble bathroom, with a double vanity, a glazed shower cubicle, an old school kidney-shaped Jacuzzi and two further doors. The vanity was strewn with cosmetics, the mirrored cupboard doors open, behind them a chaos of tubes, tubs, pots, packs, bottles and medication packaging.

On a bath stool next to the shower lay a damp, black towel, in the Jacuzzi another. Underwear and clothes hung over the edge of the tub. There was no toilet. It must be behind one of the two doors.

Allmen tried one at random. It opened only half way. A piece of furniture was standing just behind it. He slipped past it into the room, switching on the light.

This was not a restroom, but a room the same size as Jojo's bedroom. And it had clearly once been a bedroom, sharing the bathroom with the other. Now it was a gallery.

The light Allmen had switched on came from a series of simple glass vitrines, one of them placed in front of the door. Like aquariums, they were grouped around a solitary leather armchair in front of which was a small glass table.

What they contained was a collection of Art Nouveau glassware: vases, lamps, bowls. It was immediately clear even to Allmen, who knew precious little about Art Nouveau, that they were the work of the legendary Émile Gallé.

Allmen was not worried he would be caught. They were alone in the house. Jojo had assured him of that in the hall. So he took the time to have a proper look, pausing for longer at an especially fine group of pieces.

They were five bowls shaped like wide, open goblets. Their glass ranged from totally opaque to semiopaque, in shades of creamy gold, rust, ice, snow, cinnamon, silver, licorice and cacao. They were each decorated with a large dragonfly. All were golden eyed, all different, but all of them looked as if caught midflight in the glass while it was liquid.

Every one of the five pieces was perfectly executed, breathtakingly beautiful.

Allmen tore himself away, switched off the light and returned to the bathroom. He tried the other door and found the toilet.

14

He lay on his back staring with one eye at the molded plaster ceiling, dimly lit by the night light. Jojo, whom he now thought of as Joëlle again, was still snoring. He had tried to turn her on her side twice. The first time she had emitted a groan, stopped snoring briefly, then turned onto her back again.

The second time she had shaken him off, hitting his right eye with her elbow. He had to get up and bathe his eye in cold water to stop it from swelling up. Now he was lying with a damp cloth over his eye, cursing Joëlle, Lauber and himself.

He would have left ages ago if it hadn't still been pouring rain, and if he'd known where he was. He'd been so busy on the way here fighting Joëlle off, he hadn't paid attention to the journey.

According to his phone it was just after three when he decided he would leave anyway. Somewhere in this house there must be an envelope, a magazine or something with the address on it.

He gathered up his clothes and went into the bathroom. His eye didn't look good. It was red and already swollen.

As he dressed, his rage at the slut, as he now called her, increased. He looked in the mirror, saw his crumpled, lip-stick-smeared shirt, saw his swollen eye and felt like a gigolo thrown aside without his pay.

Instead of returning to the bedroom and leaving the house from there, via the corridor, he opened the door to the glassware collection, wiping both door handles clean with a dry cloth. He cleaned the light switch too, and turned it on. Without thinking twice, he went straight to the vitrine with the dragonfly bowls. It was locked, but the key was in the lock.

He opened it and took out one of the bowls. The finest, in his view. Against a milky background, the dragonfly stood out in caramel brown, its body black as a vanilla pod and its wings the color and texture of tortoiseshell. The stem of the bowl formed a sapphire bead at its widest point, divided at four regular intervals by large, white-marbled pearls of glass. The piece sat, cool and heavy, in Allmen's hand. He locked the vitrine and wiped his prints away.

Back in the bathroom he wrapped his loot in one of the black towels, turned off the light and returned to the bedroom.

She was lying on her side now, and had stopped snoring. Allmen tiptoed toward the door. As he passed the bed she sat up and stuttered, "What, what, what?"

Allmen started.

Then she said, "Ah, okay," and fell back into the pillow.

She was lying on her back again. Allmen waited till he could hear her snoring. Softly, he left the room.

15

In her haste, his hostess had left all the lights on. The corridor and hallway were fully lit. Her life-threatening stilettos stood on the steps, and in the center of the foyer, like a green beast slain for its skin, was her mink. A little farther away, flung less elegantly than her fur, was his cashmere coat, sunk in on itself like an old sack.

Allmen looked for an envelope with an address on the coat stand, where the mail was normally placed in such houses. Nothing.

The doors leading to the other rooms were all closed. He didn't want to open any of them and turn on the lights in case he could be seen from outside. Who knew, there might be a staff house out there from which you could see into the villa. And without light he would find nothing in a strange house.

The villa was on the road winding around the lake. This was almost certainly called *Seestrasse*—Lakeside Avenue. He just had to find out the house number. That would be at the door to the house or at the gate to the property.

He opened the heavy front door. Thick beads of rain glittered in the light which poured from the foyer. In the shelter of the porch he searched for a number around the door, on the pillars and frame, in vain. It must be on the gate.

Allmen put his coat on and took an umbrella from the holder by the coat stand. He looked for a spot to leave his black towel bundle, then decided to bring it, to be on the safe side.

The raindrops thundered down onto the umbrella. Allmen crossed the gravel driveway and found his way toward the gate in the dim light. It was at least fifty yards from the house and was not locked. There, on the right-hand pillar, half hidden by a cypress hedge, was the number, white on blue enamel: 328b.

The road, almost certainly Seestrasse, ran straight as an arrow to the left, to the right it curved away inland, out of sight. From here headlights now shone, approaching fast and flooding the curtain of rain in blue halogen light.

Allmen ducked behind the hedge and waited till the car had raced past.

This brief intermezzo brought Allmen back to reality. What on earth are you doing? Have you gone crazy? Are you planning to slip out of the house with a stolen Gallé bowl hoping not to be caught? Tomorrow they'll notice the theft and you'll be the only suspect. Have you taken leave of your senses, Fritz?

Allmen always called himself "Fritz"—as his father had called him—in these rare moments of self-rebuke.

Allmen stood for a moment longer, hidden in the cypress hedge under the pouring rain and thought about it. Then he pushed the black bundle in among the dense cypress branches and went back into the house.

16

Allmen woke up alone in a strange bed. The sheets were satin, the light of day filtered by opaque curtains, the space next to him still warm. It didn't take him long to recall the events of the previous hours.

The bathroom door opened and Allmen watched through half-closed eyes as Jojo—as he now returned to calling her for tactical reasons—entered the bedroom, rested, refreshed and preened. He closed his eyes completely. She opened the curtains energetically. He heard her footsteps approaching. He felt her weight on the mattress. He smelled a new perfume.

"I swore you'd be gone by the time I woke up."

Her lips felt soft, her lipstick smelled of expensive makeup.

17

One hour later they were sitting beside each other drinking coffee at a table with space for twenty-four guests, in front of them the remains of an overgenerous breakfast they had not done justice to; butter, honey, preserves, orange juice, sliced meats, eggs, muesli, bowls of fruit, salmon and a cheese board. A domestic employee had served them and then withdrawn. She came only if Joëlle pressed a small remote placed next to her plate.

They were in the villa's dining room, windows opening out onto a veranda, the garden and the lake. It had stopped raining, but the clouds were still lurking low, reflected gray-black in the water.

The room was tastefully furnished, as was the whole house (except for Joëlle's room). The owner's penchant for Art Nouveau could be seen everywhere. The villa itself was also from this period.

Joëlle's father was Klaus Hirt, the businessman. Allmen had discovered this much already. Via his enterprises, Hirt controlled several of the country's major financial companies. He never appeared in public himself, and when he appeared in the media, it was always with a photo showing him as a middle-aged man, which he had long since ceased to be.

Allmen had never met him, but he now knew they had roughly the same build. The clean shirt fit him. The collar was just a little loose. Joëlle had handed it to him saying, "Keep it. My dad has hundreds of them."

"I can hardly wear a shirt with the initials K. H." Allmen had objected. "I have initials of my own."

"Then throw it away. Or clean your shoes with it."

The late morning light was not sympathetic to Joëlle's makeup, which did not blend with her complexion as it had last night in the Golden Bar, at the opera house, in the limousine and the bedroom. It contrasted with it. Application, structure, pigmentation and transitions were all evident, like a painting you had got too close to. And yet she still looked good. It was her charisma, the charisma of someone in a good mood, happy even. Allmen suspected this might have something to do with him. Not him as a person, more the fact that he was still there the next morning. Not necessarily something which happened to Jojo often.

There were frequent, long breaks in the conversation throughout their breakfast, the kind of silences which for couples often precede confessions, announcements and declarations of love. Allmen intervened each time with a deliberate banality to rob the silence of any deep significance. This time he hit out with, "Lovely house, I must say."

Jojo reacted more crossly to Allmen's rhetorical sabotage each time, like a cat deprived of its mouse. "Too much Art

Nouveau if you ask me. I can't stand the sight of it anymore, but daddy is addicted to the stuff. He can sit for hours trying to hypnotize a vase. At least two women left him because of it. I can hardly blame them."

"Gazing on beauty is a meditative act," Allmen said thoughtfully. The statement provoked Joëlle to leave another significant pause.

Allmen checked the time. "I'll order a taxi. I have an appointment." He took his phone out of his top pocket, but Joëlle put her hand on his.

"I'll take you."

"That's very sweet, but you don't need to."

She kept her hand on his and looked him in the eyes. "Oh I need to alright. That way I get a bit more of you."

This was not part of Allmen's plan at all. That way he would be seen to leave the house empty-handed, true, but he would need both hands in the back of the limousine, under the furtive gaze of the chauffeur in the rearview mirror, to fend off Jojo's advances.

18

Allmen was not a driver. Although he had once learned, and still possessed a driver's license, folded up small and no longer legible along the creases, he believed that to drive yourself was just as degrading as carrying out any other kind of work which someone else would do better if you paid them.

For this reason he did not own a car. But for the task he faced tonight he could not delegate the driving. Which was why he was now at the wheel of a black Smart he had borrowed from a friend.

Driving a vehicle yourself was ludicrous enough; the vehicle itself shouldn't be a joke too. And the way he was driving, his back hunched over, hands clamped neurotically to the wheel, was just shameful. But he hadn't had much choice. The Smart was the only vehicle his friend could spare, a former university chum who had founded an advertising agency after dropping out of college. "You won't want to give it back," he had assured Allmen, handing him the key and getting into his Porsche Cayenne.

Now after a humiliating trip through the city center, he was driving down the endless road along the lake. Joëlle had given him the villa's address. He had asked her when they stopped at the gate to Villa Schwarzacker. She took this to mean that he wanted to visit her again; she let go of him, and didn't insist on coming in with him briefly. "But you must show me your villa some time," she had said in parting.

It was a dry night, but pitch-black. The dense, low blanket of cloud hanging over the city and its outskirts refused to budge. It was two in the morning, scant traffic. He had already passed number 200. The properties were getting larger, the numbering more erratic. The last sign he'd been able to make out was 276. Since then he had passed several entrances with no number, glimpsing gables through mature trees, flags, avenues of poplars.

A car with its headlights on full beam came around a bend from the opposite direction too fast. Allmen tried to flash a reprimand, but instead switched on the windshield washer. The water, the wiper fluid and the lights turned the windshield into a blinding white, impenetrable surface and forced him to slam on the brakes. It was awhile before he could see or drive again properly, and when he saw number 362 in the light of his headlights, he realized he had overshot by a long way.

He turned around at the next opportunity, and drove at close to walking pace back past the properties, looking carefully for house numbers.

At last he came to number 330. This must be the house next door.

A pair of headlights came toward him and flashed. The car signaled, and disappeared behind the hedge. Joëlle's

Mercedes limousine. As Allmen passed, the electric gate was closing itself.

He drove on a little, turned in a driveway, switched the lights off and waited. Five minutes, ten, fifteen. The he drove back and stopped outside 328b.

The next bit went quickly: out of car, over to hedge, grab towel bundle out of the hedge, back into car and off.

PART II

19

Allmen was still sleeping when Carlos brought in his tea. That was not remarkable as it was five to seven in the morning. Carlos started his gardener's job at seven.

Carlos was from Guatemala. Allmen had met him shortly after his father's death while he was visiting a friend who lived with his parents in Antigua, in a colonial villa with several beautifully planted patios. A neatly dressed, polite gardener, one day Carlos approached Allmen and asked him, in so many words, if he could come back to his country with him. Allmen had just acquired the Villa Schwarzacker and was killing time till the renovation was finished by travelling through Central and South America. This was the last stop. The villa would need a gardener, and he agreed on the spur of the moment. Carlos applied for a passport and accompanied Allmen on a tourist visa. If he proved himself, Allmen would organize a residence permit for him. That was the deal.

Carlos did prove himself, but Allmen had underestimated the residence permit thing. After three months he was reluctantly forced to take his gardener to the airport and bid him a sad farewell. In three months' time he would fly him back over again to stay another three months.

A couple of hours after this farewell Carlos was standing at the door to the villa again. He hadn't gotten on the plane, and was in the country illegally from this point on. He was given board and lodging in the gardener's cottage and paid four thousand francs a month—half this sum allowed his large family back home to live comfortably.

Over time, as Allmen's financial situation became increasingly precarious and he employed ever fewer staff, Carlos's workload increased. In the end he was not only the gardener; he cooked, served, ironed, cleaned, repaired, improvised, lied for Allmen and became ever more indispensable.

On the evening when he confessed to Carlos that he would be selling the villa, moving into the gardener's cottage and would have to part from him, he simply nodded and said, *"Muy bien, Don John,"* then withdrew to the cottage.

But next morning, as Allmen was sitting at breakfast and Carlos was pouring him more coffee, he said in his formal manner, *"Una sugerencia, nada más."*

This was not "just a suggestion," quite the opposite. When Carlos said this, it meant he would outline a detailed plan from which he would not be dissuaded. This time it went as follows: Allmen would negotiate for him to work as gardener and caretaker for the new owner and he, Carlos, would move into the attic at the gardener's cottage and continue working for Don John.

Allmen liked the idea. He could keep his indispensable Carlos, without paying the four thousand each month, which he'd cheerfully agreed to at a time when he had been more independent financially. He included the sum in his negotiations for the gardener's cottage, as a flat fee to be paid for gardening and caretaking. After some initial resistance, the K. C. L. & D. Trust agreed to this condition too, so keen were they to acquire the prestigious Villa Schwarzacker.

From this point on Carlos worked for his boss for board and lodging. Between the gables of the gardener's cottage were two attic rooms for staff and a tiny bathroom to go with them. Depending on Allmen's financial state, Carlos also received bonuses: tips varying in size.

Allmen finished his tea and placed the cup back on his bedside table. Normally he would now lie back and doze off again for an hour or two. The dreams at this time of the morning were the most intense. And he had no appointments in the morning except the one with himself at ten in Café Viennois.

But this morning he got straight up after his tea. He hurried in the bathroom, dressed with the usual care and soon after eight he was in the library. The large room was filled with milky light, mist rising from the lawn and shrouding the contours of the trees.

On the carpet in front of one of the shelves was a pile of books. Allmen had removed them in the night to make space for the glass bowl. He had thrown the wet towel into the half-full trash can himself, taken the plastic sack out, tied it up and left it by the door for Carlos, who would dispense with it later.

And there it was, the dragonfly bowl, in the mist-softened morning light. Even more enchanting, even more mysterious than in the vitrine of its rightful owner.

A reasonable reward for services rendered.

He sat down at the piano, placed a dead cigarette tip between his lips and bashed out a few tunes from his songbook repertoire. A ray of sunshine slipped through the curtain of mist, found its way through the treetops and for a brief moment lit up a slender column of dust.

Allmen was pleased with himself and the world.

20

"Réservé" signs were placed on the tables used by the after-ten regulars, to prevent the occasional new customers from sitting at them.

Allmen was sitting happily with his second coffee, idly glancing through a newspaper straightened in a wooden holder. The review of *Madame Butterfly* was glowing, and now he realized how little of the performance he had taken in.

Out of the corner of his eye he noticed a new customer had entered and was approaching the old man three tables away who, as always, was occupying all four chairs.

Allmen looked up from his newspaper to observe the scene. The new customer had his massive back turned to Allmen, and was standing as if rooted to the spot in front of the regular. He, in turn, had begun freeing up a chair in disgust. Gianfranco was busy with the coffee machine, and hadn't noticed this outrageous incident, otherwise he would have come to the rescue.

Now the man turned round and sat down, legs wide apart.

Dörig!

Allmen felt the tension at his chest again, which came with sudden reminders of suppressed unpleasantness. He nodded in fright at Dörig, but he didn't react. He just sat there in his tight, buttoned up coat and stared at him. A living reminder of payment due.

Allmen turned back to his newspaper, but he could sense the steady gaze of his creditor. He was aware of Gianfranco approaching the table and leaving again after a brief, quiet exchange of words, busying himself at the Lavazza then returning shortly afterward with a drink.

Dörig didn't react, didn't touch the cup, just kept staring.

Allmen raised the newspaper slightly and peeped over it occasionally. The unpleasantness had stayed where it was. And with it the tension in Allmen's chest.

Twelve thousand, four hundred and fifty-five francs. Once he would have spent that much in one night on hotel suites, plane tickets, entertaining at a decent restaurant. And now the sum was making him tense, making his heart race, his hands sweaty.

Final deadline Wednesday. What day was it? Monday?

Now there was some movement at the table. Gianfranco was standing there, being paid it seemed. He walked away again. In contempt.

Dörig stood up and left the café. Allmen watched him through the window.

As if Dörig could sense his gaze, he stopped abruptly and turned his head.

Allmen couldn't prevent their eyes meeting.

21

A dining table with six chairs, hemmed in by an Art Deco sideboard in matte-lacquered black, took up most of the space in the living-dining room. In the rest a sofa and two matching armchairs (the other two were stored in the laundry) were crowded around a coffee table, all of them American Art Deco, which had once been among his many passions as a collector.

Again it smelled of Carlos's favorite food as Allmen entered the room. This was Carlos's way of saying he needed more housekeeping money.

Once the food was on the table, Allmen realized how urgent the warning was. There were no mince patties, not even guacamole. There was just beans and tortillas, the food of the poor in Guatemala.

He consumed it without comment. Carlos made no comment either. But the way he served it, with the best dishes and cutlery on starched damask, said all that needed to be said.

Allmen was unable to sleep for his siesta. He stared at the ceiling trying to banish the image of Dörig, that tight ball of aggression. Allmen realized he couldn't palm him off with anything—except money. But he needed the small amount he had to mask the reality of his situation. He couldn't afford to use it to pay off debts.

A quarter of an hour before he normally woke from his siesta, he got up, went to the library and sat at the baby grand—replacement value around eighty thousand francs.

He played a few of his desultory chords at first, but then took some music down from the bookshelves and played a Chopin nocturne, haltingly at first, then with increasing confidence. He felt as if he had never played so well. As if he were playing for his life. Or perhaps for the life of his piano.

After the final bars he sat for a moment, lost in thought, placed the felt cover back on the keyboard, closed the lid and walked to the bookshelf where the dragonfly bowl stood. In the golden light of this late fall afternoon, it too was a thing of incomparable beauty.

What was it worth? Certainly more than anything he had offered Tanner till now. His gut told him that with this piece he had entered a whole new league.

Had Joëlle's father noticed the theft and reported it? And if he had, wouldn't the police have sent photographs to all the art and antiques dealers?

He did something he had planned never to do: he called Joëlle.

"All alone in that great big house still?" he asked when he heard her voice.

She misunderstood this and said, "Even if my dad was here, you could still come over. He's not old-fashioned."

He wasn't sure what to say to this. She added quickly, "But he's not here."

Allmen had found out what he wanted to know, and looked for a noncommittal way to end the conversation. But it wasn't that easy to escape.

"Men," she said, "who are still there the next day, then call the day after, are either after my money or smitten with me. Judging by your lifestyle it can't be the money."

It would not have been a good strategy to disabuse her, and he went as far as to invite her to Promenade the following evening, although his credit situation there was strained to the limit already.

22

"I think I have something rather special for you, Jack."

Allmen opened the case, took out a toweling bundle, unwrapped the dragonfly bowl and placed it on the polished surface of the desk.

Tanner looked at the bowl, then at Allmen, then back at the bowl and said, "Sit down."

Allmen settled down on the sofa and crossed his legs.

Tanner carefully picked the bowl up off the table, examined it from all sides, touched it softly with his fingertips and looked at Allmen.

"Gallé," Allmen said.

Tanner raised an ironic eyebrow. "You don't say."

"I used to collect the odd bit of glassware," Allmen said.

Tanner looked up from the bowl, scrutinized Allmen, lowered his eyes back to the object and murmured, "Used to collect the odd bit of glassware. Is that so … ?"

The room was filled with silence again. Allmen heard the sedate ticktock of a pendulum clock with an inlaid face. Tanner lit one of his flat Egyptian cigarettes, whose exotic aroma Allmen had noticed immediately as he entered the sacristy.

"What do you want for it?" he asked straight out.

"Jack ..." Allmen replied, "... I really can't recall the price I paid back then ..."

"Twenty thousand." Tanner didn't hesitate for a second.

Allmen, however, needed a little time to think. "I think," he said finally, "that is somewhat less than I paid back then."

"Entirely possible. But with collectors' items of this type there are often objects of dubious provenance in circulation. There are only a few passionate collectors who will buy this kind of thing without asking questions."

"And I guess their identity is a professional secret."

"Your guess is correct."

If he had prevaricated for just a moment, Tanner might well have raised his offer. But haggling was so totally beneath Allmen's dignity he agreed immediately. "It's a deal," he said. "This will help me through a short-term liquidity issue, otherwise I would never consider such a sale of course."

Tanner pulled out a desk drawer, clearly open at the back, as far it would go, and reached right inside the desk. His head disappeared. Allmen made out a metallic snapping and clicking, and after a while Tanner reappeared, closed the drawer and counted twenty thousand-franc notes onto the desktop.

Allmen patted them into a wad like a practiced card player and slipped them nonchalantly into his top pocket. He stuffed the towel back into his pilot's case and waited for Tanner to accompany him to the door.

"Should you have any more such dragonflies in your little collection, I would be interested," Tanner said as he left.

Allmen hailed the next taxi. "Do you have change for a thousand-franc note?" he asked as he made himself comfortable in the backseat.

23

As he did every time he got hold of some money, Allmen did the rounds.

He paid his bill at Promenade, settled his account with the barman at the Golden Bar and went for a coffee at Viennois, dealing with the outstanding payments and leaving a breathtaking tip for Gianfranco. He called on his florist, his hairdresser and his bookshop. All this in Herr Arnold's Cadillac, which he had himself driven home in. After he had settled that account too, he reinforced Herr Arnold's faith in his creditworthiness with a more than adequate tip.

Carlos kept neat accounts of household expenses in a book in one of the kitchen drawers. Allmen consulted it and determined that he owed Carlos over four thousand francs. He placed two thousand-franc notes in the book. Paying off the whole sum would have brought his balance dangerously close to the figure Dörig was demanding.

Allmen didn't intend to contact him. Now that he had money, he could cheerfully wait for Dörig to get in touch. He was looking forward to the moment when he could reach casually into his top pocket and hand him the sum without affording him the dignity of a second glance.

Allmen spent the rest of the afternoon reading in his glasshouse library. Black clouds gathered and forced him to switch his reading lamp on early.

24

The Golden Bar was filled with the muffled commotion of the cocktail hour. Allmen was on his second margarita, waiting for the arrival of "La Joëlle" as he was now calling her.

He was sitting at the far end of the bar as usual, where three aging loners typically sat, trying to chat with the barman, who had stationed his large red wine there. Allmen knew all three and exchanged small talk with them, between the coming and going.

One of them was Kellerman, a wasted alcoholic who carried it off with style, retired ophthalmologist, widowed for over twenty years.

The other was Kunz, a lawyer with a solo practice also functioning as the honorary consulate for the Republic of Surinam, where calls were mostly taken by a sputtering answering machine.

The third was Biondi. He owned a store selling golf equipment and belonged to Jack Tanner's daily breakfast club at Viennois.

Allmen had saved the stool next to him with his coat, for Joëlle. Kunz seemed to resent him for this. He kept looking at the coat, then at Allmen as if forcing him to explain. But Allmen resisted the pressure to justify himself and kept silent.

Kellerman was highly loquacious however:

"When did you last have your eye pressure tested?"

"My eye pressure?" Allmen had never had his eye pressure tested, was unaware eyes could be under pressure, how this might be measured or what the consequences might be if it were too high or too low.

"You're over forty, I believe," Kellermann said.

Allmen nodded.

"Then you should have your internal eye pressure tested. Just to be on the safe side."

"Safe from what?" Allmen asked, worried now. He had a slight tendency toward hypochondria and every new front which opened up in the battle for his health gave cause for concern.

"Glaucoma," the aging eye doctor murmured.

"It puts you in a coma?" Kellermann's voice was already somewhat slurred by now.

"Glaucoma. Optic nerve damage. Field of vision loss."

Allmen automatically touched his right eyelid.

"You don't feel anything. Once you start to notice, it's too late. Only one thing you can do: eye pressure and optic nerve tests every year after forty." Kellermann finished his Red Label, heavily diluted with lukewarm water, and gave the bartender a sign with the empty glass. "I'm an old man, believe me."

Allmen looked into Kellermann's reddened, watery, sad eyes. "Is the test painful—unpleasant, I mean?"

"More pleasant than tunnel vision." Kellermann took his fresh whisky and filled his glass to the brim from the little jug of tap water the bartender had brought along with it.

Biondi, sitting next to Kunz, looked along the bar, turning past his neighbor, past the stool bagged with the coat, past Allmen, to Kellermann. "A customer of mine has tunnel vision. Golf pro. Thirty-nine. Fit as a fiddle."

Before answering, Kellermann attempted eye contact with Biondi past the three stools, leaning back dangerously. "Isn't always the intraocular pressure. Can be a lack of oxygen to the optic nerve papilla. Can be. Not always, but it can be." Kellermann righted himself using the golden rail at the bar, took a gulp of whisky and repeated. "Not always, but it can be."

Thanks to this conversation, Allmen and the three men had missed the arrival of La Joëlle. Suddenly she was standing in a cloud of heavy perfume next to Allmen, waiting for him to help her out of her mink—petrol blue this time.

"Surprise!" she laughed.

"And what a pleasant one," Allmen responded chivalrously, removing his coat from the stool and helping her onto it.

"We're not going to Promenade."

"Ah, but I reserved a table." Allmen stood uncertainly in front of her holding both the coats.

"And I canceled it. Can I have a Bloody Mary? Actually on second thought a Manhattan. Bloody Marys fill you up. That would be a pity."

One of the bar staff freed Allmen from his role as lackey, taking the coats from him. Allmen sat down next to Joëlle and waved the bartender over.

"Have you ever been to shaparoa?"

One of the newest, most fashionable restaurants in the city, shaparoa—the initial letter *s* was lowercased in the first of many of this establishment's affectations—was also undoubtedly the most expensive. Its opening had come after Allmen's financial heyday. He had never been there. "Not really my thing," he said vaguely.

"Oh, don't be so fuddy-duddy." The bartender brought her Manhattan. She drank it in one go, fished the maraschino cherry out by its stalk and swung it around. "I've reserved us a table."

Allmen jumped. "But I thought shaparoa was booked up months in advance."

Joëlle threw her head back, dangled the cherry above her mouth, opened her red lips and slowly lowered it. Before she had quite swallowed it, she said, "Depends who you are."

After another Manhattan, Allmen signed the check and helped Joëlle into her coat. Kunz, Kellermann and Biondi watched. Whether with envy or schadenfreude, he couldn't tell.

25

The staff at shaparoa were dressed like the crew of the Starship Enterprise: bodysuits in high-tech artificial fibers, with stand-up collars, Velcro fastenings, in a range of colors depending on their role and hierarchy, with sneakers in matching shades. They all wore headsets, to keep in touch with the kitchen and the head of service.

He was a large, shaven-headed man, whose tight spandex bodysuit emphasized a body its owner clearly subjected to many hours in the weight room. His eyebrows were carefully trimmed and inclined upward, and Allmen would not have been surprised if his ears were pointed.

He greeted Joëlle like an old friend, calling her "Jojo." She called him "Vito" and introduced Allmen as "John. Almost the same as me, but with just one *Jo*." She put a proprietary arm around Allmen as she said it.

There was a room for each course at shaparoa, which the publicity described as a "revolutionary gastronomic concept." Vito escorted them into the *"Amuse Bouche."*

The room was decorated with toys, tiny clown figures, music boxes and cartoons. Balloons floated on the ceiling and the cushions on the seats were amused faces.

"Same as usual?" Vito asked.

Joëlle glanced at Allmen. "If I may?"

He nodded, and soon the sommelier was opening a bottle of Taittinger Comtes de Champagne Rosé 2002, at four hundred francs.

It wasn't the food which threatened to bankrupt Allmen—the culinary journey through the nine thematically decorated rooms cost him a mere three hundred and fifty francs per person—it was the drinks. As if wanting to put her date's solvency to the test, Joëlle ordered the highlights of the wine list. Even before they had left the *"Amuse Bouche"* she had ordered another bottle of champagne, then returned it barely touched.

In *"La Mer,"* a room lined on three sides by aquariums full of tropical fish, she ordered not one but two bottles of Chavalier Montrachet, Grand Cru "Les Demoiselles" Louis Latour 1997, at six hundred and eighty francs a bottle.

She had herself accompanied through the remaining rooms by a Burgundy, the La Tâche Domaine de la Romanée Conti 1995, at one thousand, four hundred francs a bottle.

In *"La Pâtisserie,"* a salon decorated entirely in pink, turquoise and silver, they asked for the check, sated and, in Joëlle's case, extremely drunk. It had come to five thousand, six hundred and seventy-three francs.

"Oops," Joëlle gulped, and smiled impishly at Allmen.

They didn't know him here. He wasn't creditworthy. He had no choice but to reach nonchalantly into his top pocket and place the sum, plus a five-hundred-franc tip, on the pink tablecloth.

Joëlle ran her somewhat unsteady hand through his hair and purred, "Men who still pay with real money are *so* sexy."

26

The chauffeur had a name now: Boris. He was practiced at dealing with his boss in this state, and stowed her gently and carefully into the back of the limousine. Then he opened the other door for Allmen and gestured with his head for him to get in. His look was reproachful, as if Joëlle's companion was responsible for the state she was in.

Boris did not wait for the outcome of the destination discussion—Joëlle wanted "your place," Allmen did not of course—and headed straight for the lakeside villa.

This time Joëlle was restrained throughout the journey. Perhaps it was the amount she had drunk, but perhaps it was that she now viewed Allmen as something with a long shelf life she didn't have to gobble up all in one night. She snuggled up against him, but didn't fall asleep.

The house was brightly lit. At the entrance there were several high-end cars in the color of choice this fall: black.

"You said you were at home alone." Allmen sounded anxious.

"All I said was that my father wasn't here."

"And who are all these people?"

Joëlle shrugged her shoulders. "No idea."

"The house is full of people, and you don't know who they are?"

"Friends of my brother's."

"So your brother lives here too?"

She shook her head. "He just has parties here sometimes."

Boris came with her into the foyer. The coat stand was covered with coats, and from the wide corridor leading to the large salon came the sound of talking and laughter. Joëlle was very unsteady on her feet now, and Allmen hoped Boris would help him out.

Which he did, leading her on past the staircase to a walnut door which disguised an elevator. "First floor," he noted apathetically, and closed the door.

27

The bedroom was lit by the two dimmed bedside lamps, with their immense silk shades. The quilt had been pulled back on both sides, and something silky and lacy had been draped on Joëlle's side. It looked like a room in a five-star hotel made ready for the night.

There was still no trace of Joëlle's rapacious sexual hunger from the other night. She waved at him like a small child and disappeared through the bathroom door. "See you in a minute," he heard her say before the door closed behind her. He heard her lock it.

Allmen sat in an upholstered chair which reminded him of the furnishings in "La Pâtisserie" at shaparoa. He was tired and had drunk far too much. And over the last few hours he had blown about half the money he owed Dörig. The thought kept flashing up in front of him, however hard he tried to suppress it. Worse: someone else had blown it.

Dörig kept appearing among the filler-thoughts from every area of his life he was using to try to block his head. Thickset and short-necked with red hands, he muscled his way in, like a lout barging into a packed elevator.

Perhaps he could appease him with half the sum.

If he still had that much.

He didn't want to count the money out now. That would be an invitation for the man to invade his head completely.

Primitives like Dörig could easily be palmed off. With half, with a third. As soon as they saw some money they found it impossible to say no. Better the bird in the hand. That's what they were like.

One disadvantage: he would have to speak to him. Not just speak: negotiate. He couldn't just thrust the notes into his hand and wave him away like an annoying fly.

But Dörig wouldn't get violent. People like that didn't get violent toward those who were giving them money and might give them more. Even when they owed them money. They just didn't.

Or did they?

Allmen had to admit he didn't actually have any experience with this type of person.

He heard sounds from the bathroom. Rushing water, clattering, footsteps, a whirring electric toothbrush. And through the other door waves of distant laughter from below.

What was taking her so long in there? Was she freshening up? Was she making herself pretty? Was she changing into something seductive? Allmen wasn't wholly unsusceptible to that kind of thing. Not slutty underwear, that was too cheap. But classy lingerie, that was easy on the eye. Even if it was on a woman who got on his nerves.

Did she get on his nerves? Not all the time.

He was starting to convince himself she was endearing again, or at least acceptable.

The door opened and Joëlle entered. She was wearing an oversized pair of men's pajamas and had cleaned her makeup off. She smiled dozily at him, got into bed and patted the pillow next to her. "Don't be long."

Then she switched the light off on her side.

28

The same chaos as last time filled the black bathroom. The clothes she had been wearing lay in restful communion with the towels and wash cloths scattered across the floor, on stools and in the Jacuzzi. The trash can was surrounded by used makeup-remover tissues which had missed the mark. An electric toothbrush was left in the sink, an open tube of toothpaste on the glass shelf with a long string of paste dangling from its opening.

Allmen searched for another toothbrush head. He wasn't suddenly finding her so endearing he wanted to use hers. He found one next to the charger.

Standing at the sink with the vibrating toothbrush in his mouth, avoiding his reflection, his eyes fell on a bubble pack of pills, two of them gone. Allmen took them from the edge of the basin and turned them over. "Rohypnol, 1mg" was written there.

Next to the sleeping tablets was a glass with a little water left. Its rim held a trace of lipstick. The same maraschino cherry she had been wearing that evening. Jojo seemed to have no further plans for the night.

29

Once again Allmen was lying in this strange bed next to this strange woman. A fall storm had built up and was whistling through the poplars lining the banks of the lake. The wind had swept the sky clear, and the moon, nearly full, cast a pale strip of light onto the carpet.

He could still hear occasional sounds from the party below.

He dreamed of his father. He was driving through a cloud of dust down the track to the farmhouse, honking the horn. Allmen recognized the car. It was the nearly new, cream Opel Kapitän his father had bought the day he signed the sales agreement for the Schwarzacker.

He was driving with his left hand. With the right he was pressing the horn and waving through the open window. Allmen stood, a small boy, at the front door to the house and watched as the car approached. Then he was suddenly sitting in the passenger seat next to his laughing father. Then he was behind the wheel driving toward his father, who was standing at the door laughing.

Allmen tried to brake but there were no brakes. So he honked.

He woke with a start. But the honking hadn't stopped. It sounded as if it was coming from the ground floor.

Joëlle was breathing regularly and heavily into his ear. He flicked on the bedside lamp. She was lying in the same position she had fallen asleep in. Her mouth was slightly open and her eyelids weren't closed tight either. The honking continued.

"Joëlle," he whispered. Then at a normal volume: "Joëlle!" She gave no reaction.

Allmen held her right shoulder and shook her. No reaction.

The honking still hadn't stopped. Now it was at a different pitch. Allmen got up, went to the door to the corridor and opened it softly.

He closed it behind him, stepped cautiously to the head of the stairs and looked down into the entrance hall. A man of around forty was standing at the open front door waving. He was answered by a car's horn, and another, at a different pitch.

Allmen heard the cars' motors grow quieter, and then louder, as they passed through the gate to the road and accelerated.

At last it was quiet. The man, presumably the brother, shut the door and turned round. He wore a fading smile, now twisting into a yawn.

Allmen drew back from the stairs, but didn't return to the bedroom. He heard the brother humming to himself. A door opened, the guest bathroom, judging by the watery sounds which soon emerged from the open door. The toilet was flushed, the door shut and then he heard the clattering of a hanger on the coat stand.

Allmen took a few steps forward again, and caught the brother in his coat at the front door before everything went dark.

The door was pulled shut. Gradually Allmen's eyes got used to the darkness. Now he saw there were emergency lights, glowing close to the floor in the hall, and by every other step along the staircase.

A motor started up, grew louder, quieter, louder again, then faded away.

Allmen was chilly in his T-shirt and boxer shorts. He returned to the bedroom and slipped in next to Joëlle under the comforter.

Now he was wide awake.

30

An hour later he was still awake. The storm had ended as abruptly as it began. Joëlle hadn't moved at all. And Allmen's head was full of dragonflies.

"Should you," Jack Tanner had said, "have any more such dragonflies in your little collection, I would be interested."

There had been five there, each one finer than the next.

They were alone in the house. And Joëlle was sleeping like a log.

The house had been full of guests. Any of them could come under suspicion.

Except for him. He would be witnessed leaving the house empty-handed. As before.

Twenty thousand.

That would solve the Dörig problem. Which, strictly speaking, Joëlle was responsible for.

Who would have thought twenty thousand would one day be an issue for Johann Friedrich von Allmen.

He got up quietly and dressed.

31

The smell of cold cigar smoke hung in the room. Allmen pushed past the obstruction in front of the door. The vitrines lit up. On the small glass table in front of the solitary leather armchair was an ashtray with a cigar butt and three intact cylinders of ash, almost identical in length, left by a very measured smoker.

Allmen walked over to the vitrine with the dragonflies. In the spot where the bowl he had taken had been, was another.

If he hadn't known otherwise, he would have sworn it was the same one.

But as he did know otherwise, he concluded the bowl he had walked off with was not in fact unique, and that was why Tanner had paid him such a low price for it.

He opened the vitrine, took the piece out and wrapped it carefully in a towel.

He did the same with the other four. Which hadn't been his original intention. But if that one wasn't unique, then the others undoubtedly weren't either.

32

Carrying a misshapen bundle of towels under his arm he walked softly down the stairs. The foyer smelled of the guests who had left the house an hour ago. Perfumes, nicotine and the exhalations of a long evening.

The door was one you could open only from the inside. Allmen propped it open with a coat hanger so it couldn't shut and lock him out.

The driveway lay in front of him, brightly lit by the moon. He took the long way around, under the protection of the trees to the hedge and along it to the gate. There he stashed his booty at the same spot in the cypress hedge he had used last time.

He returned to the house the same way. As he reached the corridor on the first floor he thought he heard footsteps. But inside the bedroom Joëlle was still lying exactly as he had left her.

He undressed quietly and slipped under the sheets. He noticed only now that he was shivering. He attributed it to the cold fall night.

33

He was woken by the whining of a vacuum. For a moment he thought he was in a hotel.

Then he remembered the previous night. The extraordinary restaurant, the extravagant wine, the exorbitant check. And the stupid thing—the indescribably stupid thing—he had done.

He pressed the palms of his hands against his eyes, as if this would undo the mistake. What devil had talked him into stealing all five bowls? Someone had obviously been in the room since his last visit, had smoked a whole cigar in peace. Why had this fact not dissuaded him from making such a blunder? The alcohol. It must have been the wickedly expensive alcohol. He had been reasonably sober, but only when compared to Joëlle. Compared to his usual drinking levels, he had seriously overdone it.

Generally Allmen succeeded in ignoring unpleasant realities for as long as it took them to vanish from his consciousness, not forever, but long enough for him to generate some pleasant realities. But this time it wasn't working. He was forced to try the second best method: opening his eyes and busying himself, thinking of nothing except, for example: now I'm pulling back the covers. Now I'm turning on my side. Now I'm putting my left foot on the ground. Now I'm raising my head while I put my right foot on the ground. Now I'm sitting on the edge of the bed.

He opened his eyes. The strip of moonlight on the carpet had given way to a glaring band of sun. The mother-of-pearl boudoir of the night had been transformed into a tasteless bedroom.

Still fast asleep, Joëlle had undergone a similar metamorphosis. Her face was slightly bloated now. Here and there shone the remnants of her thickly plastered night cream, and on her lower lip a thin red wine crust could be traced, which had withstood the removal of her makeup.

Allmen stood up and went into the bathroom. He found some towels in a cupboard and took out more than he needed. He showered and distributed the towels around the bathroom, so that the ones stuffed into the cypress hedge would not be missed.

He shaved with a lady's razor he found in one of the mirrored cabinets, and got dressed.

Joëlle was still sleeping when he returned to the bedroom. He had no choice; he would have to wait till she woke. He needed her as a witness he had left the house empty handed.

It was just after ten thirty. He had to do something to accelerate her waking process.

Allmen went to the window and opened the curtains. The room filled with merciless sunlight. But Joëlle showed no sign of waking.

Perhaps he should bring her breakfast. Always a reasonable excuse for waking someone.

He headed out into the corridor.

The vacuum had been silent for a while, but there were sounds coming from the ground floor. He descended the staircase.

The foyer had been tidied up and aired. In the corridor that led to the living rooms stood a cleaning trolley and a vacuum. Allmen walked to the door at the end where he hoped to find the kitchen.

It was the pantry. The food was served from here, sent up in a dumbwaiter from the kitchen.

The room was empty. But the door to the dining room was open. Allmen entered.

The table was laid for two people. There was a third place, which had been used. The domestic worker from last time, a middle-aged woman in a gray and white striped apron, was busy clearing the plate, cutlery and leftovers onto a tray. Now she paused and looked at him.

"Good morning," Allmen wished her.

The woman nodded and smiled faintly.

"Do you think … I would like to bring Frau Hirt's breakfast to her room. Do you think you could assemble a few things she likes to eat?"

The woman nodded again and continued clearing the place at the table. She took the tray into the pantry. Allmen followed her. She took a fresh tray from a rack and returned to the table. Allmen followed her back and saw her gather up the crumbs with a table sweeper then clear one of the place settings and put everything on the fresh tray.

"Coffee?" she asked. She had an accent but Allmen couldn't place it with just this one word. He hesitated. "While I prepare Frau Hirt's breakfast?"

Polish, Czech, somewhere in that region.

"Do you have espresso?"

"Double?"

"Double." Did he look that wasted?

She gestured to the chair in front of the remaining place setting at the table. He sat and waited. After a short time she returned with the espresso and a newspaper.

Only the smell in the room revealed that a few hours ago there had been a huge gathering. There was a very mild aroma of cigar smoke in the air, mixed with a dry, leathery eau de toilette.

Allmen skimmed the headlines then turned to page three for an article trailed on the front page.

From where he was sitting he could see the double doors out to the corridor. And from the corner of his eye he now noticed a figure passing by.

When he looked up the person had gone, but before he had time to turn back to the newspaper, he returned. As if he had noticed the man at the table in passing and wanted to check he hadn't been mistaken.

The figure was Klaus Hirt. He stood in profile, half hidden by the door frame, his head turned toward Allmen, and mumbled something which sounded like a greeting.

And then he was gone. The cigar smell was stronger than before.

Now Allmen uttered a greeting in return—if the nervous coughing sound he projected toward the empty doorway could be described as a greeting.

So Hirt was here! It was Hirt who had smoked a cigar in the glassware room. It was Hirt's footsteps he had heard in the supposedly empty house. He might easily have met him earlier. He might easily have bumped into him in the glassware room. He might easily have been caught in the act by him.

He would definitely leave the towel-wrapped bundle in the hedge alone now.

The domestic worker came in with a tray. It contained two espressos, a glass filled with a green liquid, a glass of water on a saucer holding two Alka-Seltzer tablets and a half-bottle of champagne. "Frau Hirt's breakfast." She said this with an entirely straight face.

Allmen attempted to take it from her with the same matter-of-factness.

34

When he returned to the room, the bed was empty. The bathroom door was ajar, and inelegant sounds were coming from within: coughing, choking, spitting, groaning, swearing.

Allmen placed the tray on the bedside table and considered how to make his presence known.

But at that moment the door flew open and Joëlle entered. She was naked, which he noticed had suited her better in the gentle silky light of the other night, than the glaring sunshine of this warm morning, with the foehn wind blowing.

It took a few seconds for her to notice him. "Shit! I thought you'd gone." She looked down at herself, shot him a look of hatred and rushed back into the bathroom.

When she returned, ten minutes later, she was wearing lipstick, eyeliner, a little makeup, one black towel as a turban and another as a sarong.

Now she saw the tray. She headed straight for it, peeled the two Alka-Seltzers and dropped them into the glass of water. She watched in fascination as the tablets jumped around in the commotion of their carbon dioxide.

"You've saved my life," she murmured, and patted his cheek.

The tablets had dissolved to leave just a small deposit of white crumbs. She put the glass to her mouth and emptied it in one go with practiced ease. Then she took the glass with the grass-green liquid, drank half and said, "Barley grass juice. Detoxifies the body and strengthens the immune system." She sat on the edge of the bed and drank the first espresso.

"I saw your father."

"Oh, is he here?" In a disinterested way she sounded surprised.

"You didn't know?"

"With my father you never know where he is at any one moment. Come here, sit down. You can have my second espresso."

"Thanks, I already had mine." Allmen sat down next to her. "I'll have to be going soon."

"Could you open this baby for me?" was all she had to say to this announcement.

Allmen uncorked the small champagne bottle and filled the flute.

"First the other espresso." She held the empty cup out as if he were a waiter.

He swapped it for the full one, its brown froth already clearing to reveal a circle of dark liquid.

She drained the cup, screwing her face up, and held it out to him. He took it from her and placed the champagne glass in her hand, still outstretched.

Joëlle drank half the glass and placed it on the bedside table. Then she threw her arms up in the air, stretched and yawned. "Boris will drive you. Whenever you're ready."

"Now then." Allmen said bluntly.

She went to the telephone, dialed a short number and said, "*Ja*, Boris. Herr von Allmen is ready to leave. Thank you." She put the phone down and smiled at him. "He'll be waiting for you in the drive."

Joëlle held her left cheek out to him, and put a hand on his neck. With the other she patted his cheek again, in the same patronizing way. "Thanks," she murmured, "it was nice."

Allmen walked down the staircase, wondering why she had brushed him aside so unceremoniously. He consoled himself by concluding she felt he had seen too much of her. Too much reality, in too much light.

Boris was waiting for him with thinly disguised mirth. As they left the gateway behind them, Allmen muttered, "See you never again, Jojo."

35

Around midday Allmen pressed his doorbell.

"Hello?" came Carlos's voice, suspicious.

"Soy yo," Allmen answered.

"Don John ..." he heard Carlos say, then the line was cut and the buzzer sounded. Allmen took the section of the path toward the villa then turned off down the smaller path to the gardener's cottage.

The door was open, as always, and Carlos was waiting in the vestibule. Allmen could see immediately something was wrong. Without waiting for his greeting, Carlos said, *"Don John, le esperan.* You have a visitor."

"Who is it?"

"Un señor." He gestured toward the living room with his chin.

Before he even saw him, Allmen knew who was waiting for him; he was standing in the half-open door. Now he opened it fully. Without a word he held his open hand out to Allmen. When Allmen failed to react immediately, he waved it up and down, demanding.

Allmen managed to get his coat off, with Carlos's help, before reaching into his top pocket for his remaining money. He counted out five thousand-franc notes into Dörig's paw.

Dörig stood still as a pillar of salt and waited for the rest.

Allmen looked through his pockets, found two hundred-franc notes and a fifty and placed them with the larger notes.

Dörig said, "Twelve thousand, four hundred and fifty-five."

"Do we have any more money in the house, Carlos?" Allmen asked casually.

Carlos went into the kitchen and returned with the two thousand-franc notes Allmen had slipped into his household accounts. Allmen placed them on the immobile, outstretched hand.

Dörig waited.

"The rest will follow in the next few days," Allmen said firmly.

Dörig turned his hand ninety degrees. The notes fell to the ground. "No one palms off a Dörig," he said quietly and menacingly. Then he placed his right heel on the arch of Allmen's foot and shifted his entire weight onto it.

Allmen yelped.

"Friday. Same time. Same place. Or else …"

Dörig went to the door and stood there. Carlos got the message and opened it for him. Dörig handed him a tip of ten centimes. Carlos closed the door behind him, threw the coins in the trash can next to the coat stand and bent down to gather up the notes from the floor.

Allmen was hopping on one foot, rubbing the other.

"No one palms off *a* Dörig!" he kept muttering in disgust. "*A* Dörig!"

36

It wasn't often that Allmen could not be distracted by a book. He was under no illusions that his hunger for literature had really always been his way of avoiding this reality by barricading himself in another.

But this time the barricades were not withstanding the onslaught. He was reading *A Woman of Thirty* by Balzac, an author he could normally rely on to transport him into another world. But even Balzac couldn't block out the images of the last day.

Joëlle kept slipping in between the lines. Effusive and decadent at shaparoa, later a weary, needy pajama girl, then hungover, naked and spent in the late morning light, finally cold and haughty as he left. And the dragonfly bowls kept appearing, in their finest light in the vitrines, and as an ungainly bundle of black towels in the cypress hedge.

The image of Klaus Hirt kept getting in his way too. The way he had peeked through the door in passing. What kind of look had it been? Searching? Disparaging? Suspicious? Knowing?

And when he succeeded in banishing these images, another barged its way past Balzac's elegant counts and refined marquises, the crude and vulgar Dörig. *A* Dörig!

That man was the hardest to suppress. Thanks to the dull pain of the bruise on his foot he was omnipresent. Allmen had taken his shoe off and raised his leg and was putting his faith in the ointment Carlos had prescribed. It came from a battered metal tube labeled *"Milagro"*—miracle.

Allmen gave up. He put the book aside and hobbled over to the glass wall facing the rear of the grounds from where you could see the dark thicket behind the greenhouse, where the urban fox sometimes appeared.

If he were honest, a rare situation in Allmen's life, he would have to admit he'd pretty much hit rock bottom. No, not pretty much. He had hit rock bottom. Period.

He was living from hand to mouth. Superficially easing his most urgent debts no longer hid even to himself that something much bigger was building up behind them, which would sooner or later crash down on top of him. The goodwill he had gained during his years of extravagance would soon be exhausted. All the well-disposed creditors would turn, one after another, into a swarm of Dörigs, dominating first his thoughts and dreams, and then his reality. Nothing could save him.

Except a bolt from the blue.

37

Carlos's parents sent him out onto the streets at the age of four as a shoe-shine boy. They bought him a rough, wooden shoe-shine box, painted black. At the beginning it went very well. He wasn't terribly skilled at polishing shoes yet, but he was so small and cute he often fought off the competition for the few tourists who wore leather shoes, not sneakers. Some gave him ten quetzals instead of the standard price of one. And occasionally one would buy him something to eat from a snack bar at the side of the road.

But as he got older he needed to excel at the craft. He worked on becoming the best shoe-shine boy in the town, concentrating on regular local trade: officials, policemen, store owners. Carlos conjured up the brightest of shines on a pair of shoes, and cultivated a virtuoso technique with his brushes and polishing cloth. His customers would actually look up from their newspapers or interrupt a conversation to watch the little stylist among the shoe-shine boys perform.

Carlos had maintained these skills and cultivated them to this day. When he polished Allmen's extensive collection of shoes he insisted, with that polite impertinence of his, that the shoes be on Allmen's feet. After refusing initially, Allmen had eventually got used to sitting in his glass library on the raised piano stool, one foot on Carlos's black shoe box, while he polished his shoes—with the drapes closed, naturally.

He switched feet automatically at the sign from Carlos, a rapid tap on the tip of the sole, and reluctantly put another pair on while Carlos put shoe trees in the freshly polished pair.

This ritual was almost the only opportunity to discuss things beyond the usual household questions.

"Carlos, is it alright to do something dishonest when you are in trouble?"

"*Cómo no, Don John.*"

"*Cómo no*" was Carlos's way of saying yes. It meant more than yes. It meant, "of course," "naturally," "damn right." The answer came quickly, like most of Carlos's answers. It was as if he kept a stock of ready-made answers he could call on as needed, to all the questions of life.

"If there's nothing honest you can do to get out of trouble." This qualification didn't please Allmen. Nor did the following: "But only something dishonest. Not something criminal."

Allmen watched him for a while, as he whizzed over the toe cap of his black handmade English shoe with the taut polishing cloth, giving it a whack every third time. In all the years Allmen had never found out how he made that noise. "What would you do if I went to prison?"

Carlos looked up from his work. "That would be terrible, Don John." But after a while he said. "Although it would be less work for me."

Allmen turned back to his Balzac.

38

The college friend who had lent him a Smart last time, now gave him a BMW. It smelled of new leather and was full of electronics Allmen didn't understand. On the dashboard was an illuminated map displaying his journey and his current location. Allmen didn't like the idea that he was constantly being tracked by a satellite. Probably it would be possible later to retrace exactly where he had driven tonight.

It was just after three. Allmen had chosen this time because he reckoned it was the hour after the late-night party people went to sleep and before the early risers awoke. And sure enough there was very little traffic. Above all on this suburban road which ran along the lake.

He concentrated on driving the car. He had caught himself exceeding the speed limit twice already. The vehicle was so quiet and finely tuned Allmen had no sense of what speed he was going.

Concentrating on driving had the advantage that he couldn't question the decision he'd come to. It was as if someone else had taken control of him and he, Allmen, was just their proxy.

There was still a foehn; it was mild and dry. The moon was full and made the night bright and clear. He would have preferred a few heavy clouds.

Very occasionally a car came the other way, and two or three times one overtook him. Once he had to brake for a cat, and at one point he passed a pedestrian wearing a windbreaker with reflective strips, which caught Allmen's headlights from a long way off. The villas stood still and dark along the shore of the lake.

As he approached number 328b he dropped his speed even further. The light above the front door was off, but the windows were giving out a weak light. Probably the night lighting in the foyer and on the stairs, which Allmen was familiar with of course.

He drove a few houses on and turned in an entranceway. Then he drove back and left the car opposite the next property. He waited a few minutes, got out and walked along the hedge to the gate.

He could see the spot with the bundle of towels from a distance. It stuck out slightly from the hedge. He'd shoved it in that carelessly—thanks to the state he'd been in. Amazing no one had discovered it.

Just as he was removing it, the light above the front door came on. Allmen ran back to the car, as fast as he could with his injured foot, placed the loot on the backseat and started the engine.

He had been driving only five minutes when Hirt's limousine overtook him, Boris at the wheel, driving fast.

39

On the way into the city he met a police roadblock. He saw it from some distance. He was waved over with a red-lit traffic baton. A uniformed officer came over to the car and waited by the driver's door for Allmen to open the window.

Allmen didn't know how to do that. He fiddled with the various buttons attached to the door but the window remained shut.

The officer called a colleague over. Allmen attempted to explain using gestures that he wasn't familiar with the vehicle.

Now the first officer reached for his pistol holster. The other was trying to open the door. But there was an automatic safety lock mechanism which prevented the vehicle being opened from the outside. Allmen raised his hands above his head.

He saw one officer say something to the other, laughing, before taking his notebook and writing something on it. "Switch the motor off," Allmen read, as the officer held the note against the window. He did as told and the officer opened the door.

"Not my car," Allmen confessed right away.

They asked him to get out. The officers shined their flashlights inside the car. Both beams of light rested on the black towel bundle on the back seat.

Allmen's heart raced. The officers exchanged glances. Then they switched their flashlights off and turned to Allmen.

They checked his papers and the papers for the BMW. They ordered him to renew his tattered driving license within fourteen days. Then he had to take a Breathalyzer test. He just passed: 0.4 per mill. The wine he'd drunk with dinner must still have been in his system.

Eventually they let him go. "Zero point zero, zero per mill would be better," they advised, "when you're driving an unfamiliar vehicle."

He promised to stick to this in the future and drove home slowly and with extreme care.

40

Earlier Allmen had refused to own a computer for aesthetic reasons. When he needed anything for which a computer was required there was his office. Yes, in the good times, he'd had an office. Anyone calling his number was answered by a woman's voice saying, "Johann Friedrich von Allmen's office?" with the accent on the A. He had a secretary deal with his correspondence, book his travel and look after financial matters. After the fall of his empire, as he sometimes called it in a mood of ironic self-deprecation, he had delegated these tasks as far as possible to Carlos.

Carlos owned a computer, which he used mainly to keep in contact with his family in Guatemala. He had an ink-jet printer too, and paid for the Internet connection.

And the next day it was also Carlos who photographed the five dragonfly bowls. He was a keen still life photographer, since in the days when he had looked after Allmen's orchids, he had also photographed them as a hobby.

On top of the piano he positioned a sheet of pale gray photographic background card in a curve and photographed the five bowls assisted incompetently by his boss.

Carlos climbed up into his attic and returned proudly ten minutes later with the results. The milky light of the cloudy day, and the small spotlight Allmen had been required to direct at the objects, had created images of a more or less professional quality. Only the cheap ink-jet printer left something to be desired.

Allmen put the pictures in a folder and the folder into a small leather briefcase while Carlos cleared away the photographic setup.

Now the five Gallé bowls stood in all their glory on top of the piano, reflected in its black shiny surface. They both gazed at them thoughtfully.

"Don John, una sugerencia, nada más."

"Yes, Carlos?"

"It might be better if they didn't stay here."

Allmen looked at him askance. "You're afraid they might be stolen?"

"They look valuable."

"They are valuable."

"And the whole room is made of glass."

"What's your idea, Carlos?"

"I'll take them to a safe place."

"Where then?"

"When you need them, Don John, I'll bring them."

Allmen reflected. "Agreed, Carlos. I'll let you know when I need them."

41

It got dark early that afternoon. The thin sheet of mist had thickened during the day to a thick blanket of fog. It had turned cold too. Allmen had left the house in his raincoat, but returned immediately. Now he was wearing a woolen overcoat, scarf and gloves.

In the shop windows there was already light, and the sensors on the streetlamps had also decided it was nighttime.

Only in Les Trouvailles was it dark. The timer switch must be set for a later hour. But why hadn't Jack Tanner switched the lights on himself? He must be there. Allmen had made an appointment.

He pressed the doorbell and heard it ring inside. But there was no sound of footsteps on the creaking parquet, which normally came immediately.

Allmen left a little pause, not to seem impatient. Then he rang again.

Still nothing moved in Les Trouvailles.

It was only now that he noticed that the door wasn't closed as normal, but was slightly ajar. He could push it open without pressing the door handle.

Which he did, and called, "Hallo? Jack? Are you there?"
Silence.

Allmen tried to push the door shut behind him, but it didn't catch. Then he remembered that Tanner always had to lift it slightly so that it shut properly. He tried this now, and it worked.

It smelled different. There was the aroma of old furniture and wax polish as ever, but another odor was mixed with them. Something Allmen recognized but couldn't name.

"Jack? Are you there?"

Everything was quiet. The only sound was the creaking parquet floor as Allmen walked to the back room.

There the strange odor was more intense. It was coming from Tanner's tiny office, the door to which stood half open. Allmen knocked politely on the door frame. "Jack?"

He walked in.

Jack was sitting with his back to the entrance, on General Guisan's revolving chair. His head was tilted back, like someone asleep on a train.

"Jack?"

Suddenly Allmen realized what the odor reminded him of: the hunting trips his father had dragged him on when he was little. This is what it had smelled like when he fired his shotgun, making little Fritz cry over yet another rabbit or partridge.

He took a few steps around the desk. Far enough to see that Jack Tanner was missing a chunk of his forehead, his face a grimace of clotted blood, mouth gaping wide.

Allmen ran. Out of the office, through the storeroom, through the display room and out onto the street. It was only then that he realized how stupid he'd been. He should have stayed there of course, and called the police.

He tried to go back into the shop. But this time he had instinctively shut the door the way he had always seen Tanner shut it. The lock had caught and it couldn't be opened from outside any more. He tried the handle a few times. Hopeless. It wouldn't move.

He was about to reach for his cell phone to call the police. Then he thought of his briefcase.

His briefcase! With the photographs of five stolen Gallé bowls! Was he going to invite the police to look at that?

"Have you tried the doorbell already?" a voice said behind him.

Allmen jumped. An elderly lady carrying a shopping bag was giving him a friendly look.

Allmen nodded. "Several times."

"Then Herr Tanner probably isn't there. He often isn't. Do you have an appointment?"

"Ah, is it by appointment here?"

"Most people make one. Otherwise … well you see how it is."

"Thanks for the tip." Allmen turned to go.

"You have the number?"

"Emm …"

"Best to write it down." The woman pointed to the glass panel in the door. A business card was fixed to it.

Allmen took his gloves off. Only now did he realize he'd had gloves on the whole time. He took a ballpoint and a notebook out and wrote down the number.

The lady nodded, pleased, walked to the neighboring door and fished a bunch of keys from her purse.

Allmen put his notebook away and sauntered past her. "Thank you and good afternoon."

42

Carlos had lit the wood stove and pulled one of the leather armchairs closer to it. Allmen sat wrapped in a blanket shivering. Carlos was crouched next to him holding a cup of steaming liquid.

"Drink it while it's hot, Don John," he said.

Allmen reached his hand out, but it was trembling too much. Carlos put the cup to his lips. Finally Allmen drank, in small, cautious sips.

To make this grog Carlos had sacrificed some of his twenty-year-old Guatemalan rum, which he had been given for a birthday years ago and never opened, so concerned was he about Allmen's condition.

The latter had returned home earlier than normal, white and silent. "*Todo bien, Don John?*" Carlos had inquired.

Allmen had nodded. And the nod had turned into uncontrollable shuddering. Since then he had just been sitting there, and wouldn't say a word about why he was in this state.

But the grog and the fire and perhaps also the words of comfort began to take effect. Allmen relaxed. The shuddering now came only in short bursts, at ever greater intervals.

Once it had subsided completely, and Allmen had drunk the grog, he offered Carlos the other chair.

"I prefer to stand, Don John."

Allmen had given up resisting Carlos's obsequiousness. Over time he had come to realize that Carlos felt happy in this role. He was pretty certain it actually gave him a sense of superiority. But for what he wanted to say now, Carlos could not stand next to him like a lackey. "Sit down!" he ordered.

Carlos did so, with an obedient *"Muchas gracias."*

"Carlos," he began.

"Qué manda?" Carlos asked. This Guatemalan expression, literally "what is your command?" had unnerved Allmen at first until he discovered and accepted it was just a meaningless idiom.

"Carlos ..." Allmen looked for an appropriate way to begin. Their relationship had always been respectfully distant. Although they had lived under the same roof for years, friendship had never developed between them. Complicity sure. But not friendship. Carlos had a keen sense of the distance, physical and emotional, which he believed was appropriate between them. If Allmen breached it Carlos knew exactly how to reinstate it. This time—for the first time—he let it go.

"Carlos, I have to tell you something."

Carlos nodded and waited.

And Allmen described his visit to Jack Tanner, and the condition he found him in, and his ill-judged flight. He left no detail out.

Carlos listened attentively. When Allmen was finished, he got up. *"Ahorita regreso,* be right back."

Allmen heard him climb the stairs and after a minute come down again. He was carrying a transparent file folder holding various sheets of paper. He sat down and handed Allmen one of them.

It had the letterhead of the St. Gallen Cantonal Police and showed the five dragonfly bowls, all in professional studio shots. Beneath this was a text revealing that these were the most famous of the works stolen nearly ten years ago from an exhibition of Gallé glassware. They had been lent by a private collector.

Their value was estimated at several million francs.

The insurers were offering the sum of four hundred thousand francs for information leading to their recovery.

Allmen looked up from the sheet and met Carlos's searching look. "I never knew that," he murmured.

Carlos said nothing.

"Where have you put them?"

"When you need them, Don John, I'll fetch them."

43

He woke soon after four a.m. from an uneasy sleep and tried to doze off again without success. The image of Jack Tanner rose from the darkness each time.

Had someone found him? Or was he still sitting at his desk like a grotesque specter?

As soon as he succeeded in banishing thoughts of Tanner, the dragonflies took their place. Were they genuine? Or were they fakes? If they were genuine, why were there two of the first one?

Shortly after five he heard Carlos's footsteps above him, heard him in the bathroom, heard him come down the stairs, heard him clattering about in the kitchen.

Was he right to have confided in him? Could he really trust him implicitly?

Suddenly it hit him with full force: four hundred thousand francs reward! That would keep Carlos and his family in Guatemala comfortable for the rest of their lives! One phone call to the police would be enough. He would have a few problems with the immigration authorities to deal with, but the worst they could do was make him leave the country.

With four hundred thousand francs in his pocket that would be bearable. Above all when you considered the alternative here: two jobs, only one of them paid. And a boss he often had to support.

Allmen leaped out of bed. He had to get the dragonflies out of the house, as soon as possible.

In the shower he put a plan together. He would pack the bowls in a suitcase with a few clothes and toiletries, and take the train to some random destination. There he would leave the suitcase. Perhaps in a locker. Or with left luggage. Or in a self-storage unit. He would improvise. The plan had another advantage: he wouldn't be at home when Dörig appeared.

But the plan came to nothing. Allmen emerged from his room to ask Carlos for the dragonflies, already packed and dressed like an Irish country gentleman in a tweed suit with suspenders and a waistcoat, but Carlos was already gone. It was only half past six, half an hour before he normally started work, but he was gone. The table was set for breakfast. There was a note left next to the plate. In his childlike handwriting Carlos had written, "*Muy buenas días,* Don John, I have to run an errand. There is tea in the thermos and the coffee machine is prepared. Just switch it on and it will make the coffee. *Disculpe,* forgive me—Carlos."

Allmen poured himself a cup of tea. What kind of errand had driven him out of the house at this hour of the morning? What could be so important he couldn't even bring him his early morning tea?

He would have to wait for Carlos to return. He had no idea where he had hidden the dragonflies. Without his help he would never find them.

Assuming they were even in the house.

A feeling of helplessness swept over him. He pushed the teacup aside, went into the kitchen to the coffee machine and pressed "on."

Soon a humming sound began, and grew louder. But it seemed forever till the water boiled, the kitchen filled with the aroma of coffee and the dark liquid came through the filter, first in drops then in a stream.

He took the full pot of coffee out of the machine and went back to the breakfast table. As he crossed the vestibule, he saw a bulky figure approaching the front door. Dörig.

The door was flung open, as if the owner had come home.

"You're up early today," he said, seeing Allmen fully dressed. His took in the suitcase, which stood by the coat stand. "Travel plans, I see."

Allmen pulled himself together enough to come out with: "I was expecting you later."

"That's one way of putting it," Dörig smirked, pointing at the suitcase.

Then he stretched out his hand with the same demanding gesture as last time and stared at his debtor, lowering his forehead.

The only reaction Allmen could muster was a helpless shrug.

"No?" Dörig inquired sarcastically.

Allmen shook his head.

Dörig opened the front door and called, "Okay guys, do your worst!"

Three burly men in overalls came in. They were holding ropes and straps.

Allmen was paralyzed. He watched the men approach and closed his eyes.

But no blows came, no kicks, no pain. Their footsteps continued, first thumping over the floorboards then muffled by the carpets in the library.

Allmen opened his eyes hesitantly. He was alone in the vestibule. Nervously he walked into the living room and looked from there into the library.

Under Dörig's supervision, the three men were busy with his piano.

Abandoning himself to fate Allmen watched as they took his Bechstein baby grand away.

As he left the house, Dörig growled, "The matter is now settled as far as I'm concerned."

Allmen mumbled, "It's worth much more."

And that was the only resistance he could manage.

Allmen went back into the library and spent a couple of leaden hours in his reading chair. He saw Carlos coming and going, but Carlos didn't notice him. He abandoned himself to his thoughts, waiting till it was lunchtime. He must have dozed off. But finally he heard sounds from the kitchen. It had got darker. It would start snowing at any moment.

Allmen eased himself out of the armchair. As he passed the spot where the rear of the glasshouse faced a tall thicket of trees, he sensed something move there.

The trees grew dense and dark there, the stems of tall pines and spruce rising through an impenetrable undergrowth of yew and bracken. Sometimes Allmen saw an urban fox emerge or vanish at this spot, searching for something to eat in the gardens and forecourts of the villa district.

He stepped back, stood in front of the glass panel and stared at the undergrowth.

He felt a hard blow to his chest. As he fell, he heard a muffled thud, and sensed pain at the back of his head.

PART III

44

"**D**on John. Don John. Don John," someone was singing. Allmen opened his eyes.

"Don John. Don John. Don John." Carlos was leaning over him tapping his cheek to the rhythm.

Allmen looked around. He was lying on the floor of his library, his head resting on a cushion. Carlos was kneeling next to him.

He raised his head slightly and felt a sharp pain in his left chest. He looked down at himself and noticed his upper body was naked. To his left was a pile of bloodied tissues. Another tissue was covering the painful spot on his chest. His jacket, waistcoat, tie, shirt and undershirt were scattered to his right. The last two were also slightly bloodied.

He sat up.

"Cuidado," Carlos warned him. "Careful."

Allmen took the tissue off his chest. He was bleeding slightly from what looked like a cut.

The back of his head hurt too. He felt around and found a large lump on it. It felt moist. When he looked at his fingertips they were tinged with blood.

"What happened?" But before Carlos could answer, he remembered. "Someone shot me!"

Carlos nodded. "It looks that way."

"And why am I not dead?"

Carlos picked something up off the ground and held it up. "*Un milagro,* Don John, a miracle."

It was Allmen's left suspender. The broad strip of woven fabric was the same shade as the suit, and was attached with buttons to the pants; the suspenders and suit were from the same tailor and belonged together. The adjustable clasps were large and made of brass, with Allmen's initials etched into the outer cover—the tailor's little gag.

One of them was now badly malformed and unreadable. The cover was bent inward, and the clasp behind had come out of the hinge and stuck out now, sharp and dangerous.

Allmen understood. The buckle had deflected the bullet. The clasp had made the cut. A miracle indeed.

Supported by Carlos he struggled to his feet. The pain at the back of his head got sharper. Allmen touched the bump with his hand again.

Carlos pointed to a small side table. The impact of the bullet had thrown Allmen off balance. He had fallen back and banged his head on the little table, which had made him lose consciousness briefly.

There was a small, clean bullet hole in the glass. The dark green undergrowth looked threatening.

Allmen drew the drapes. The movement caused a stabbing pain in his chest. He felt the area around the wound. His ribs were sore from the force of the bullet.

"Un milagro," Carlos repeated, and genuflected.

Allmen's legs gave way. Carlos propped him up and led him to the reading chair then wrapped him in a blanket.

Allmen blacked out.

When he came to there was a fire burning in the wood stove. All the drapes were closed and the standing lamp was giving out its comforting glow. Allmen was wearing a t-shirt and a cardigan. No idea how Carlos had managed to put them on him.

"What time is it?"

"Nearly five."

"Don't you have to work, Carlos?"

"I took the afternoon off."

Allmen burst into tears. "My nerves," he sobbed. "It's my nerves."

Carlos patted him awkwardly on his forearm.

Gradually Allmen pulled himself together. The awareness he had narrowly escaped death receded to the background and another rose in front of him. "Where are the dragonflies, Carlos?"

"In a safe place, Don John. When you need them, I'll get them."

"I may need them soon."

"Then I'll bring them soon."

"Tell me where you've hidden them."

"In the piano, Don John."

45

Carlos never made jokes. And Allmen stared in horror at the place where a few hours ago his Bechstein had stood.

He looked at Carlos, sitting stiffly on the edge of the leather armchair, an impassive expression on his face.

"In the piano?" Allmen repeated in disbelief.

All of a sudden Carlos's face stretched into a broad grin. Then he revealed his two gold capped front teeth and laughed.

Allmen joined in hesitantly. But then he was gripped by a fit of hysterical giggles. He held the painful spot on his chest and laughed, choked, coughed, laughed some more and slapped the alarmed Carlos repeatedly on the thigh.

Once he had calmed down and composed himself, like a long-distance runner still breathing heavily after reaching the finish line, Carlos said, *"Don John, una sugerencia, nada más."*

"Sí Carlos?"

"A veces hay que luchar." Sometimes you have to fight.

46

That same evening Allmen moved to a hotel. It had become too dangerous to live in the gardener's cottage.

He decided on the Grand Hotel Confédération, an elegant if stuffy five-star establishment in the city center. Allmen knew the manager there. He used to run the République in Biarritz, where Allmen had been welcomed as a regular guest in his good years.

He had been intending to book a standard room but decided against it, fearing this untypical modesty could be misinterpreted and damage his creditworthiness. He booked the junior suite.

Carlos helped him pack and carry his two suitcases to Herr Arnold's Cadillac.

Allmen saw him standing pensively in front of the wrought iron gate watching the car drive off.

The journey took a mere ten minutes. Reception had been instructed to inform the manager as soon as Herr von Allmen arrived. They chatted briefly, Allmen describing the building work at his villa which obliged him to move to the hotel for a few days.

Then the manager took him in person to his suite. He had taken the liberty of upgrading him, moving him from the Junior to the Rose Suite, where Herr von Allmen used to accommodate his guests.

Allmen had never set foot in the Rose Suite, and had no idea how generously he had offered hospitality to his guests. And those had been the guests he wasn't especially close to and hadn't wanted to accommodate in the villa.

The suite included a spacious vestibule with a guest bath, a wardrobe and three doors. Two of these led into bedrooms, each with their own bathrooms, the other to a large salon with a winter garden and a view of the old town.

Allmen felt at home immediately. He unpacked his suitcases, ordered a club sandwich and a half bottle of Bordeaux and rang the bell for the first round of the fight.

47

"Yes?" Her voice sounded American and sleepy.

"Is that you Jojo?"

"Who is it?"

"John. John Allmen?"

"What time is it?"

"Seven thirty."

"Are you crazy? You're seriously trying to get me out of bed at seven thirty in the morning!"

"In the evening. It's seven thirty p.m."

"Shit." She put the cell phone down. Sighing, coughing, silence. "Half one. One thirty p.m. I'm in New York. What do you want?"

"Your father. I have to talk to him."

"I'm not traveling with my father."

"I didn't know you were in New York."

"Sorry, I forgot to ask your permission."

"How can I get hold of your father?"

"Try calling him."

"I don't have his number."

She sighed. "One moment."

He waited. Finally she returned to the phone and gave him two numbers, the landline and the cell.

"Was there anything else?" Was he imagining it, or did she sound friendlier now? Hopeful?

"No. Nothing else. Thank you."

She hung up.

48

He imagined the shrill ring of the telephone echoing through the lakeside villa. The room waiter knocked with his snack. Allmen held his hand over the mouthpiece on the old-fashioned hotel telephone and called him in.

He wedged the receiver between his ear and shoulder, signed the bill and handed the waiter a banknote. At the villa no one was answering and the ring tone gave way to a busy signal. Allmen hung up. Now he realized how reckless he'd been just calling the waiter in. How could he have known it was actually the waiter? And not the man who had nearly killed him that afternoon.

He bolted the door and dialed Klaus Hirt's cellphone number.

A hoarse male voice answered, immediately. "Yes?"

"Allmen. Is that Herr Hirt?"

"Who's asking?"

"Allmen. Johann Friedrich von Allmen. A friend of your daughter, Joëlle."

"She's away."

"I know. New York. I just talked to her. She gave me this number."

"She shouldn't have done that."

"I have to talk to you."

"Do you indeed? I don't. At my age there's nothing much I have to do."

"It might be of interest to you."

"There are very few things which are still of interest to me."

"Do they include Gallé bowls with dragonflies?"

There was a short pause at the other end. Then Allmen heard coughing and after that a clearer voice: "Even they don't interest me as much as you might imagine."

"But enough to meet me?"

"Tomorrow afternoon. Shall we say three p.m.? At my house. You know where it is."

Allmen sat down at the table where the room waiter had set out his food, took a sip of wine and started on the club sandwich. He wasn't a massive fan of club sandwiches. He had ordered it only because this international room service classic reminded him of his earlier life. When he'd had no worries, above all not financial. When he'd lived in hotels as if they belonged to him. When he'd felt safe and secure everywhere.

49

He sat with a book and the rest of the Bordeaux in the winter garden. A few floors below him the trams slid by and the heavily wrapped pedestrians hurried along the sidewalk to get in out of the cold. The bright rows of office windows began to show their first dark gaps, and low-lying mist created colored auras around the neon signs crowning the banks.

Allmen had got comfortable, taken off his tie, switched his jacket for a cashmere pullover and his shoes for the leather travel slippers he always took with him on hotel stays. He would have felt silly in the hotel's own terry cloth slippers.

Once he had turned a page his hand became still. But the trembling had retreated inside him. And there it continued, like an earthquake with its epicenter deep beneath the earth. The calm which had taken hold of him since he had decided to fight was just superficial. Like so much in his life.

He stood up abruptly, switched the light off in the winter garden and withdrew to the sofas in his salon, his heart racing. He had suddenly realized what an easy target he would be for a gunman on one of the rooftops opposite.

He suppressed the urge to quell the inner unease with a beer or two from the minibar. There was something shady about having a drink from the minibar. Like drinking bitters from your briefcase.

He had first got drunk at fifteen, visiting his parents. His father kept a stock of schnapps which he bought from neighboring farmers and gave to other farmers and local politicians he wanted to do business with, pretending it was home distilled. Fritz helped himself to a bottle from this supply, took it to his room and drank nearly a quarter of it. Straight from the bottle. Out of lovesickness.

After he had sobered up and recovered from the ghastly hangover, his father said, "It's fine to drink. But never alone."

Since then drinking alcohol had always been a public activity for Allmen. And it could be deemed public as long as one other person was involved. Even if their role was simply to pour it.

He got changed again.

Just after office hours ended, the Confédération bar became a meeting place for bankers. There they swapped work gossip, moaned about their bosses and raved about their children, who they had left waiting with the mothers.

Around seven the sales staff from the surrounding stores took over, followed by hotel guests drinking an aperitif with their dinner guests.

Then it went quiet in the Confi, as insiders called it.

Allmen sat with his second beer at the bar. There was just one bartender on duty. He was passing the time by polishing glasses, drying cutlery and wiping tables. After the movie houses and theaters closed a few more guests would drift in, not many—the bar was not directly on the theater crowd's route—but there would be a little more life in the old Confi yet.

Allmen ordered another beer. He was enjoying the sensation of being in a hotel. It was a little too close to his home, but it was so international he could imagine he was anywhere in the world.

Tomorrow he would leave this safe haven. First he would show his face at Viennois and see what people were saying about Jack Tanner. There had been nothing in the papers yet.

Then he would make his way to the lion's den. At the thought his heart missed a beat each time. But nothing could happen to him. He and Carlos had taken care of that.

Before the first of the theater crowd arrived, Allmen signed his bill. He didn't want to meet anyone he knew tonight. And there were plenty of them around this city at this time.

50

There it was again, that hotel moment he so loved: waking in the half-light of a strange room and not knowing where you were—which city, which country, which continent.

As you opened your eyes the images of the room were still like the fragments of a kaleidoscope just before they coalesce into an image and the puzzle is solved.

This time the solution was a disappointment. He was in the city he had been in the whole time recently. And the new, unfamiliar aspect facing him brought him more fear than joy.

To retain a slight illusion of being far away, he ordered an early morning tea from room service, as if he were in England, New Zealand or India.

But as he heard the knock on the door he was dragged back to brute reality. Instead of having the steaming cup brought to him in bed, he had to get up and cautiously ask "Who is it?" in English through the closed door.

"Your tea," a voice said, in English, but with an accent which left him no doubt as to his geographical location.

He put the tray down on the table, but took it straight to the bed as soon as the room waiter was gone. On it was a newspaper. In the local news section he found an item on Tanner.

The well-known shopkeeper J. T. had been found dead yesterday in his store, an established arts and antiques emporium. The police did not believe it was suicide.

A few details followed. A neighbor had notified the police after seeing various customers throughout the morning and afternoon, ringing the bell with no answer although they had appointments. This had never happened. When Herr T. was absent, he had always hung a sign on the door.

There were no clues yet as to the background and motive for the murder. Possibilities included armed robbery or a personal dispute.

51

"**B**uongiorno, *Signor Conte,*" Gianfranco said, placing a café au lait and two croissants on the table in front of Allmen. "Have you heard about *povero Signor Tanner?*"

"I'm afraid I have, Gianfranco."

"*Bestiale! Tremendo!* Nowhere are we safe in this world. *Straziante!*"

After what by Gianfranco's standards constituted a lengthy tirade, he retreated from the table.

Soon after this Tanner's breakfast club came in. The three men talked to one another with the earnestness of the bereaved and the euphoria of survivors.

Allmen got up, walked over to the table and expressed his condolences.

Shot, he was told. From behind. In the head. Executed. A silencer. Otherwise someone would have heard. Just now he was sitting on this chair. Like us. Not even sixty.

Allmen heard all this standing. The only free chair was Tanner's. And no one wanted to offer him that.

He returned to his table, drank his second coffee, ate his second croissant, signed the check, handed Gianfranco a tip and was helped into his coat then accompanied to the door by him. All as if there was no chance this might be the last time in his life.

52

The heating in the Fleetwood smelled slightly of the engine. But it was warm and cozy on the wine-red leather backseat. Dark clouds left trails hanging low over the lake. "It's going to snow," the laconic Herr Arnold had predicted.

He had also agreed to wait outside the villa for Allmen. And he had taken down the taxi sign, as he always did for Allmen.

Glenn Miller was coming through the speakers, Herr Arnold's favorite music. Before he inserted the cassette each time—the Fleetwood did not have a CD player—he asked Allmen if he minded. And each time Allmen assured him that for him too, Glenn Miller was one of the greats.

"I knew the man who was shot in his shop," Allmen observed.

"Crazy business," Herr Arnold replied. "And people say taxi driving is dangerous. You're not safe anywhere these days."

"Not anywhere," Allmen confirmed.

Herr Arnold's weather forecast was proved right. All of a sudden fine snowflakes began swirling in front of the windshield, forcing him to switch on the wipers, one of which still shuddered. By the time they arrived outside the lakeside villa the flakes had grown large and heavy.

Arnold got out and rang the bell. The gate soon started to open inward. When Herr Arnold got back in there was snow on his thinning hair and rounded shoulders.

He drove the Cadillac sedately into the drive, and took the opportunity to open the door for Allmen and accompany him to the door of the house with his umbrella.

They waited, in silence, till they could hear movement inside and a figure opened the porch door. It was Boris, the chauffeur.

Before he entered the house, Allmen gave Herr Arnold an imploring look.

"I'll be waiting," he said.

53

oris greeted him coolly and led him through the foyer to the elevator. He was a whole head taller than Allmen and stared down mutely at him throughout the short ride.

Allmen followed him down the corridor, past Jojo's bedroom to a door with a chip reader affixed to it. Boris took a card from his pocket and scanned it in.

The door didn't open, but a voice from a speaker hidden in the ceiling asked, "Boris?"

"Herr von Allmen is here."

Only now did the door open, with a soft hum. They entered, and found themselves in the room with the vitrines.

"Thank you Boris," came Klaus Hirt's gravelly voice. Boris gave Allmen one last condescending look and left the room.

"Come on in, you know your way around."

Allmen walked in past the vitrines, which were blocking his view into the center of the room.

The blinds were closed. Hirt was sitting in the modest light of the vitrines on the leather chair behind the glass table. A fine column of smoke ascended from the cigar in the ashtray and joined the fog which could be seen here and there in the light of the vitrines.

The old man wore a stretched, pilled cardigan and slippers. At his chest hung glasses on a string. He had thrust another pair up above his forehead to his distant hairline.

He gestured to the chair opposite, placed there for the occasion. Allmen sat down.

On the table was a small humidor, a bottle of Armagnac and two brandy glasses, one almost empty and one clean. Hirt shifted forward in his chair, groaning, and filled both glasses. He pushed the fresh glass over toward Allmen.

Then he flipped the lid of the humidor open and held it out to his guest. Allmen declined.

Klaus Hirt sank back in his chair. "So?"

"I would like to say something first."

"Anything you wish."

"My personal assistant ..." Hirt's amusement at this description of Carlos briefly made Allmen lose the thread. But he continued, firmly. "My personal assistant knows where I am and the purpose of my visit. He has instructions to inform the police if he hears nothing from me by four-thirty p.m."

Hirt nodded in ironic acknowledgement. "Quite right. One can never be careful enough."

Allmen refused to get annoyed. "I have come here to make you an offer."

"Fire away."

Allmen paused for effect.

"I return the dragonfly bowls to you, and you recall your hit man."

Hirt tipped his brandy glass and took a sip. "Which hit man?"

"The one who shot me yesterday."

"And how come you're still alive?"

"The clasp on my suspenders saved me."

This sentence provoked such an uncontrollable fit of laughter, and then such an alarming fit of coughing, Allmen was worried Hirt might choke.

It was some time before he could speak again. "So your suspenders saved your life. How does that feel, may I ask? Have you framed them?" He was shaken by laughter and coughing once more.

When he recovered, he became sober. "Excuse me. At the end of one's life it is sometimes difficult to be serious. So someone shot you. Do you have any idea why?"

"Because I stole your Gallé bowls."

"And how would I have known it was you?"

"You have been observing me. You found out who I was through your daughter. Or through your Boris."

The old man took a drag on his cigar and watched the smoke as he blew it toward the ceiling. "Have someone shot for five Gallé bowls," he said thoughtfully.

Now he noticed Allmen's glass was still untouched. "You haven't drunk a thing. Please drink. It's a good year. 1931. It's also my year."

"Thanks. I prefer to keep a clear head."

"That is not the easiest way to handle life." Hirt sniffed the Armagnac, took a small sip and placed the glass cautiously back on the table. "I would like to explain something to you."

"As long as it doesn't take too long. As I said, four-thirty."

Hirt waved dismissively with a tired gesture. He looked Allmen in the eye, opposite him, and began: "You are right. There was a time I might perhaps have had someone shot for these bowls. If I could have found someone who wouldn't just hit the suspenders." This time the thought provoked a mere smirk.

"There was a time—not so long ago—when I was addicted to these five bowls. For me they are the finest thing created by human hands. Believe me, there have been days when I would shut myself in this room for four or five hours and do nothing except worship my dragonflies. I would place them on this table, one after the other, then all together, then two together, then another two together. For hours."

He reached down between his thigh and the arm of the chair, retrieved a remote control unit, as used for televisions, and pressed a button.

Now the glass table was bathed in bright light. It came from tiny spotlights mounted all over the room. Hirt could dim, swivel and turn every one of them with his remote, and alter the lighting in the vitrines.

He played with it for a while, illuminating the things on the table, then plunging them into darkness, altering their shadows and emphasizing their forms.

"This was how I brought them alive, lit them up, made them glow and dance. I was in love. Yes. In love with five glass bowls."

He took another drag and another sip. "And do you know what? I couldn't share this pleasure with any other person. It was a lonely passion. But I didn't mind. Quite the opposite. That was the thrill of it. It was something which belonged to me, and me only. Herr von Allmen, you have one of those people before you, who hoard artworks which are unsellable—because they are stolen—solely for their private, personal, solitary pleasure. This is what they look like, if you had ever wondered."

Allmen had barely seen the old collector during this whole monologue. All the lights in the room were directed at the glass table between them. Only the occasional reflection from something on the table sent flashes of light onto Hirt's face.

"Love," Allmen observed, "surely love is a classic motive for murder."

"You are quite right. But only as long as the flame still burns. Mine has gone out."

"Why?"

Hirt shrugged his shoulders. "That's the thing about love. It comes and it goes. You must be aware of that. As one of the ever growing army of my daughter's exes."

He reached for the cigar, changed his mind and withdrew his hand. "Bad luck: I'm not interested in your hostages any more. You can keep them. And worse luck: I can't recall the hit man. I didn't send him."

Now Allmen did drink some Armagnac. It had the aroma of eighty long, tranquil years and tasted rounded and smooth.

"Who was it then?"

Hirt looked at his watch. "We still have enough time before your personal assistant springs into action." He refilled the glasses and leaned back.

"This summer it will be ten years since the dragonfly bowls vanished. They were in a Gallé exhibition at the Langturm Museum on Lake Constance, on loan from the Werenbusch family."

"*The* Werenbusch family?"

"Indeed. It was an act of barbarism. Do you know the museum?"

Allmen did not.

"It's a little remote, in an old mill outside town. The thieves rammed the door with an all-terrain vehicle—the investigation determined that at least—and destroyed eight irreplaceable objects in the process. They took a little more care opening the glass cubes over the five showpieces. The whole thing was over in eleven minutes. That was the time between the alarm going off and the security people arriving. The thieves have not been caught to this day. The bowls were insured for the exhibition of course. For a sum of nearly four million francs."

Klaus Hirt had a sense of timing. He took a sip from his glass and tapped the ash from his cigar. Only then did he add: "Nearly double what I paid." He watched the sentence take effect on Allmen.

"You weren't behind the robbery?"

"I would never have allowed works by Gallé to be destroyed simply to leave the impression the robbers were novices."

"But you bought the loot nonetheless."

"It was a win-win situation, as they say. For me the fulfill-ment of a dream. For the seller an incredible deal."

"Two million for less than eleven minutes work. Not bad."

"Six," Klaus Hirt corrected him.

"Six minutes? Even better."

"Million." Hirt looked knowingly at Allmen.

"Six million? Why six all of a sudden?"

"Two from me and four from the insurance."

Allmen could see in the dim light that the storyteller was smiling. Now he clicked. "You mean it was the owners …?"

Hirt nodded.

"But you said the Werenbusch family …"

"They were in a highly precarious situation at the time. If anyone had found out, it would have become much more precarious. One of the sons, a very practical and unscrupu-lous person, had an idea how they could get out of this tight squeeze, and agreed to execute the plan. It was also him who contacted me afterward. Gallé collectors know each other."

"What's his first name? I was with a Werenbusch at Charterhouse."

"Terry."

"Terry Werenbusch!" Allmen pictured an imperious, thin-lipped boy with a receding chin, three years below him.

He was expelled in the second year. He couldn't remember why right now.

"You know him?"

"I wouldn't say 'know.' You think he carried out the robbery himself?"

"I wouldn't be surprised. He's a daredevil. Grenadier officer, base jumper, hunter."

Allmen took a large gulp of Armagnac. Hirt was watching, and tried to refill the glass. His guest put his hand over it.

"Come now. You might need it."

Allmen let him refill it.

Hirt continued. "Do you have an explanation for why the bowl you stole the first time was back in place the second time?"

"Gallé made several of them. Or it was a copy."

Hirt smiled and shook his head. "Two days after you made off with the bowl, I had a call from Jack Tanner, someone you also know. Knew, I should say, sadly. He said he had something sensational for me and I invited him to come by. It was my dragonfly bowl. Tanner knew it was from the Langturm robbery and not sellable. Except to fanatical collectors such as me."

So it was Jack Tanner. Why hadn't it occurred to him earlier? "But why did you buy the piece back? Now your love had gone cold."

"If I hadn't, Tanner would have gone knocking on a few other doors, and woken a few sleeping dogs. It was worth spending the ninety thousand."

Something in Allmen's facial expression made Hirt add, "What did he pay you? Forty?"

"Fifty."

"Very reasonable. Anyway I bought the piece off him. But on one condition. He had to tell me where he had got it from. Your name was mentioned."

Allmen felt the blood shoot into his cheeks. He tried to distract from it by taking a swig out of the brandy glass. "That means, on my second visit you knew …"

"Sure. And I was here in the night, and realized that this time all five were missing."

"And yet you let me go in peace?"

"I was happy to be rid of the things. Cheers."

He raised his glass toward Allmen, but Allmen confined himself to a nod, and asked, "And who is trying to kill me?"

"This is the unpleasant part of the story." He took the cigar from the ashtray, found it had gone out, chose a new one from the humidor and lit it with practiced ease.

"After Tanner had sold me your loot, I called Werenbusch and told him the story. I wanted him to be aware there were now two people in the know. Two people who knew that at least one of the pieces was with me. I thought it was only fair. Now I realize it was a mistake."

A shiver went down Allmen's spine. "You think Terry …"

"Who else? Terry needs to prevent anyone finding out the Werenbusch family themselves were behind the robbery of their loans. It would ruin them. No doubt about it: Terry is behind the murder of poor old Tanner and the attempt to murder you."

Allmen reached for his glass, realized his hand was shaking, and retracted it. "And why are you telling me all this?"

"I am, or rather was," Hirt corrected himself, "a fanatical art collector, who would sometimes go further for my passion than the law permits. But I will not have anything to do with murder."

The spotlights which had been lighting up the table between them went out and the lighting in the vitrines went on. The two men could see each other better now.

"Do what you wish with this information. Don't worry about me, I'm a dead man."

"How am I supposed to take that?"

"I'll spare you the technical details of the diagnosis. But I will say this much. If I have anything to do with it, I will not see beyond the next week. And I do have something to do with it. I have taken measures. No suspenders will save me."

The old man laughed, and his laughter gave way to a fit of coughing. Allmen waited till it was over.

"I know you prefer to exit via the bathroom, but I've had it screwed shut. My daughter is too careless about such matters." Hirt pressed the remote and the door Allmen had entered through opened with a hum.

Allmen walked toward it, stopped and turned back to the old man. "Where does Terry live today?"

"Still at the family home on Lake Constance. The little hunting lodge his father bought during the war. He also still lives there by the way, old Werenbusch. Blind and deaf and cantankerous."

Allmen shook the sick man's bony hand. "Thank you."

In the corridor he was met by Boris. Klaus Hirt must have informed him electronically his guest was ready to leave.

Snow had settled outside. The black Fleetwood had turned white. Now the wipers began to sweep semicircles across the windshield and the car drove off.

As Allmen sank onto the backseat, he saw Herr Arnold's look of concern in the mirror. "Everything okay?"

"Everything."

54

On the way back they got caught up in the rush hour traffic, which had come to a standstill in a few places thanks to the early snowfall. Many of the motorists were still using summer tires and the traffic slowed down around abandoned cars and minor accidents.

Herr Arnold's favorite cassette was starting to get on Allmen's nerves. But it was a long-held understanding between them that they both liked Glenn Miller. Allmen didn't want to undermine it, and sat in the back in silence, watching the gray-white chaos on the streets and letting his thoughts drift.

Terry Werenbusch! Was it possible he was guilty of Jack Tanner's murder? Guilt? If this was true, guilt was clearly not something Terry Werenbusch felt.

Allmen hadn't met him since Charterhouse. He had once seen him in a photo in *People* magazine. But he had recognized him only from the caption. As an adult, Terry had grown a Van Dyke beard to disguise his thin lips and weak chin. He had also once seen him playing in a Medium Goal Polo Tournament, a daring but inelegant player with a plus one handicap.

Now he remembered why Terry had been expelled from school. One cold winter evening he had locked another boy in the equipment storeroom next to the rugby pitch. The whole school, the police and half the neighboring village had searched for him, and Terry had joined in the search zealously. The missing boy was found only in the early hours of the morning, nearly frozen to death. Terry, who had been equipment monitor that day, denied fiercely that this was deliberate. But his victim was able to persuade the headmaster the opposite. Stupidly, Terry had written him a letter a few days earlier in which he threatened, "I'll kill you, you dirty pig!"

It was nearly seven when Herr Arnold accompanied his passenger with his umbrella through the snowstorm toward the hotel entrance, handing him over to the doorman, who met them with his own umbrella.

55

That evening Carlos was wearing one of Don John's barely worn, discarded suits. Allmen passed them on to him sometimes, although Carlos was somewhat shorter. Carlos knew a Columbian asylum seeker, a trained tailor now working as an office cleaner but boosting his income with alterations and repairs. He took Allmen's suits apart and sewed them back together as if they had been tailor-made for Carlos.

Allmen had called Carlos and invited him to dinner at the Confédération. This was a first, and Carlos had reacted with appropriate surprise, trying every possible excuse to get out of it. But Allmen insisted. It was important, he explained. It was about the fight of which they'd spoken.

You could see by looking at Carlos that he didn't feel comfortable when the maître d'hôtel led him to Allmen's table.

The restaurant at the Confédération was called *Helvétique* and specialized in classic Swiss cuisine from every region of the country. It was in an elegant dining room, paneled on all four sides, full of niches and screens, decorated with engravings of people in traditional Swiss dress. The linen tablecloths were starched and every table was laid extravagantly with porcelain, silver and crystal. Even people with more restaurant experience than Carlos might have been intimidated by these surroundings.

He sat down opposite Allmen and began to study the menu. Soon afterward he placed it aside.

"Decided already?" Allmen asked.

"I'll have what you're having, Don John."

However when the waiter tried to fill his glass too— from the bottle of Dézaley standing in the ice bucket on the side table—Carlos declined. He never drank alcohol. His father had died of it, when Carlos was five and the youngest of his six siblings was two. Drowned in a ditch by the side of the road, having fallen asleep drunk, unaware of the heavy rain. One of the few personal details he had confided to Allmen.

Given the early onset of winter, Allmen ordered Emmental potato soup, *Berner Platte* and for dessert, *crème au raisiné de Vaud*.

Allmen retold the entire story of the dragonfly bowls, disclosing everything. Then they discussed their plan of attack.

They had long been the only guests left, and it was very late as Allmen took his new accomplice to the exit.

It had gotten colder and was still snowing. A snow plow with a flashing hazard light came past loudly.

As they said goodbye, Allmen added, "The moment has come when I need the dragonfly bowls, Carlos."

"*Cómo no, Don John*. Then I will fetch them."

56

Allmen had the wine-red leather seat to himself as ever. Carlos had insisted on sitting in the front next to Herr Arnold. This time there was no Glenn Miller. They were listening to a radio station with a bland mix of oldies, pop, *Volksmusik* and popular classical. Herr Arnold apologized for it. "It's for the traffic news," he said.

The situation on the roads was indeed tricky. It hadn't stopped snowing, and the further they got out of the city, there was more and more snow left uncleared.

At the moment they were on a detour to avoid a jam on the highway which Herr Arnold was informed of thanks to the *Volksmusik* and traffic news. They were driving slowly down a narrow local road through the white landscape. The fruit trees, still in leaf at this time of the year, were weighed down with the snow. It was hard to see ahead. The headlights from the approaching cars made halos in the mixture of snow and fog. The three men spoke little and stared intently out into the winter landscape, as if they were each at the wheel.

In the night, Carlos had found the address of the Werenbusch family seat, and printed it out along with a map.
He had also searched the name Terry Werenbusch online
and discovered he was managing partner of a firm called
Wereninvest.

Allmen had called there first thing in the morning and
asked for Herr Werenbusch.

He was not in the office yet, he was told. What was it
about?

A personal call, Allmen explained. They had been at
Charterhouse together, he happened to be in the area and
had something with him which would undoubtedly interest
Herr Werenbusch.

He left his name and cell phone number. In less than ten
minutes, Werenbusch called back.

"Vonallmen?" He pronounced the name with the stress
on "von," as if it consisted mainly of the first syllable. "Vonallmen? To what do I owe the pleasure? After all these years."
The cheerful tone sounded forced. Allmen sensed deep suspicion behind it.

"I don't know if it will be a pleasure. But interesting,
certainly."

They arranged to meet at the office in the early afternoon.

57

The road to the hunting lodge had not been cleared. Herr Arnold attempted to keep the lurching Fleetwood on the tracks left by other cars. They passed a couple of farms, otherwise the area seemed desolate.

The tiny road led to some woods. A couple of forest workers paused to gaze at this spectacular vehicle.

At the edge of the woods there was a turn. All the tire tracks went left. The road ahead vanished into indistinct white. There, somewhere, must be the banks of the lake.

Herr Arnold also drove left and soon the lodge could be seen, a large timber framed house with a couple of turrets. They headed for it.

It was a while before anyone reacted to Allmen's ringing. It was a young woman in the white pants and blouse worn by nursing staff in hospitals. She opened the door with the words, "There's no one here."

"Good afternoon, I have an appointment with Herr Werenbusch."

"Herr Werenbusch Jr. is in the office. And the housekeeper is out shopping."

"Then I'm sure he will be here any moment. Could we just wait till he arrives?"

The nurse hesitated.

"I'm an old school friend of Terry Werenbusch," Allmen said reassuringly.

Allmen's appearance, and the Cadillac with its chauffeur, waiting inside, seemed to inspire confidence. She opened the door wide and let them in.

They entered a hall full of hunting trophies. On either side were staircases leading to the upper floors.

The nurse took their coats and Allmen introduced Carlos. "Herr de Leon, my assistant."

Carlos put the pilot's case down and shook her hand.

"Erika Hadorn. I look after Herr Werenbusch Sr."

She led them to a small salon with a large slate table in the middle. A selection of magazines was placed on it. It was clearly here that one waited before being received.

"Is he that bad?" Allmen asked with concern.

"Well, for a few years now he's been blind. You're more dependent on care than if you still have your sight."

"Do you think it would cheer him up if I said hello?"

She hesitated.

"Just briefly. Perhaps it will remind him of the old days."

"To be honest, I haven't been here long. So far he hasn't had any visitors at all. I don't know if it would cheer him up."

"Worth a try, perhaps?"

She considered briefly. "Okay, come this way."

They followed her up one of the staircases, along a corridor to a door. Behind it was a cozy living room with a view of the lake, still veiled with falling snow. There were two vit-rines in the room, full of glassware. Vases, bowls, sculptures, all Art Nouveau. Mostly by Gallé.

"Please take a seat for a moment," the nurse said, and went into the next room. Through the closed door they could hear her talking loudly. "Visitor" they heard, "school friend," and "just quickly." She put her head around the door. "Herr Werenbusch will talk to you briefly, but he needs a moment."

Allmen and Carlos looked around the room. Both rested their eyes briefly on the vitrines. They nodded to each other.

The ringtone from Allmen's cell made them jump. It was Terry Werenbusch. "Where are you then?"

"I wanted to ask you the same question. I'm here, at your house."

"My house?"

"Sure."

"I'm waiting for you here, in my office." He sounded indignant.

"Didn't we say we'd meet at your house?"

"Certainly not."

"Do excuse me, I must have gotten confused. I'll drive over now. Could you tell me the way?"

"You take the … You know what, I'll be with you in twenty minutes."

They had to wait nearly ten of these, before Werenbusch Sr. was ready to receive. The nurse opened the door and ushered them in.

Allmen got up. "It'll just be me. Herr de Leon will wait here."

Werenbusch was sitting in a wing-back chair. He wore a suit with a handkerchief in the top pocket, a pale blue shirt with a tie, and smelled of freshly applied eau de toilette. His white hair was thick, freshly parted. His eyes gazed straight ahead, and seemed not to be focused on anything.

"Who are you?" he asked, with the excessive volume of the hard of hearing.

"Allmen," the latter shouted back. "Johann Friedrich von. I was with Terry at Charterhouse. Johnny, I was called then."

"I had an orderly once called Vonallmen. In those days officers were still given an orderly."

"That can't have been me. A little before my time." He said this in an amused tone, but it annoyed him.

"Your father perhaps?"

Allmen's father had indeed been an officers' orderly during the war, before he became a private. "I hardly think so. My father was a colonel. In the cavalry."

"I see," Werenbusch muttered. "Cavalry colonel. Vonallmen ..."

In the room stood a hospital bed, a wardrobe and a table where a game of solitaire had been started. On the walls hung oil paintings, landscapes and still lives. And between the two windows, through which the lake would be visible in better weather, was memorabilia from Werenbusch's time in the military. Photos, from recruits to colonels. Group photos from his first platoon to his final battalion. And embarrassing, homemade, farewell presents from his underlings.

"And? What do you want?"

The nurse gave Allmen an apologetic look.

"To say hello. I happened to be in the area and I have an appointment with Terry. I thought I'd pop in and see you too."

Werenbusch said nothing.

"So much snow, and it's only late October."

"I can't see how much snow there is. I'm blind."

"At least eight inches. And it's still snowing."

"I don't care how deep the snow is. I don't go out any more."

"Very wise," Allmen said cheerily.

"It's got nothing to do with wisdom. I don't have the choice. I would prefer to go out, believe me. I would prefer *not* to be blind, if you can get your head around that."

"Of course." Allmen looked at the nurse and shrugged. She nodded.

"It wasn't actually a decision I took, *let's go blind*. And certainly not a *wise one!*"

"Well, Herr von Allmen had better be going now, he does have an appointment with your son after all." The nurse stood up.

As did Allmen. "I just wanted to quickly …" He held his hand out to the blind man, and the nurse took her patient's upper arm to help him find it.

Allmen was surprised by a very strong handshake.

"Goodbye and all the best," Allmen wished him.

"Yeah, yeah," Werenbusch said.

As he was leaving, Allmen heard him mutter, "Pity."

58

Carlos was sitting on his chair just as before, the pilot's case on his knee. Now he stood up, and as the nurse left he gave Allmen a slight nod.

They were led back to the reception room.

"Terry has called. There was a misunderstanding. He was expecting us in his office. But he will be here shortly, Frau Hadorn."

And at that moment they heard footsteps on the polished wooden floor. Soon afterward Terry entered the room.

Allmen would have disliked him even if he hadn't known he had tried to shoot him dead two days ago. He felt the hairs on his neck stand up, like a dog about to defend its territory.

Terry still had the Van Dyke beard, but now it was threaded with gray. His gaunt face had acquired wrinkles, the eyes retreated into their sockets.

He approached Allmen with an outstretched hand and wide steps, stopped short as he saw Carlos, then continued and took Allmen's hand.

Werenbusch's hand was clammy.

"Long time no see," he said. Then, glancing at the table, "Has no one offered you anything to drink?"

"Frau Gerber has gone shopping," the nurse explained.

"Of course," Terry realized. "Frau, erm …"

"Hadorn." The nurse helped him out.

"Frau Hadorn is my father's nurse. Not her job to offer guests anything."

Only once she had left the three of them alone did Terry hurriedly offer Carlos his hand.

"Carlos de Leon, my assistant."

Terry closed the door and sat down at the slate table. "Please." He gestured to two chairs opposite him. They sat and for a moment there was an awkward silence.

If the number of times someone blinks is a measure of their nervousness, Terry Werenbusch was extremely nervous. Tiny beads of sweat had gathered on the bridge of his nose. Both signs made Allmen a little more determined than he already was.

He gave Carlos a sign. Carlos opened the pilot's case and took out a reddish-pink folder and slid it across the table.

Allmen put his hand on it. "I have to say one thing first. Copies of these photographs are also with my lawyer, along with a detailed account of your role in the robbery and the measures you have taken to silence the people who recently became party to information. Along with a signed statement detailing my role in the affair. He knows where we are and has instructions to hand everything to the press and the police if I don't report back to him tomorrow, in person and in one piece."

Now he released the folder.

"Does *he* have to be here?" Terry asked.

"Carlos is my personal assistant," Allmen answered simply.

Werenbusch opened the folder. It contained the photographs Carlos had taken of the dragonfly bowls. He looked slowly through them, looking several times from the photos to Allmen, then back to the photos. The pieces of paper shook slightly in his hand.

"One of them is missing," he said finally.

"Klaus Hirt bought it back."

Terry nodded and looked at Allmen. He said nothing. Waited.

"I could go to the police and claim the reward."

Werenbusch raised his eyebrows. "To the police? With things you have stolen?"

"I didn't steal them. I discovered them by chance at Hirt's house, recognized them and took them into safe keeping."

"Why don't you do it?"

"I may still. I mean, if we can't come to an agreement about my proposal."

"Let's hear it." Terry leaned back. It was supposed to look relaxed, but did not.

"Very simple. I give you the bowls back, and you give me the reward I would otherwise receive."

Allmen could see how intensely Werenbusch was thinking through the proposal.

"And what's in it for me?"

"You can hide the evidence or destroy it." Allmen paused for effect. "And that will wipe out the connection between you and us." He paused. "You and Tanner and me."

"I have nothing to do with Tanner," Terry blurted out. Allmen didn't try to contradict him. He let his proposal sink in.

Werenbusch thought about it. "And Hirt."

"He will keep quiet. He is implicated. Whether with one dragonfly or five."

Terry took a tissue out and wiped his face. "And what do *you* get out of it?"

"Without the evidence I'm no longer a dangerous witness. That's a huge relief when you live in a glass house."

Werenbusch was not convinced. "That would also be true if you went to the police. What's the advantage to you?"

Now Allmen actually smiled, he felt so sure of victory. "I would get four hundred thousand from the insurance company. From you I would get five hundred thousand."

For the first time in his life Johann Friedrich von Allmen was bargaining. In this case, and in this situation, it didn't feel so bad at all. He still hoped his opponent didn't come back with a lower offer.

But his opponent did no such thing. He pursed his thin lips, rocked his head from side to side and finally asked, "Can I think about it?"

Allmen looked toward Carlos, who had been sitting immobile the whole time. He caught the hint of a shake and turned back to Terry.

"No."

Werenbusch nodded. "How? Where? When?"

"How: we will hand over the bowls, you the money, in cash. Where: in the Seeschloss Hotel. When: is two hours enough?"

"Half a million in cash in two hours? The bank closes in one and a half!"

"What do you suggest?"

"Tomorrow. Ten-thirty. At the earliest. The absolute earliest!"

"Let's say eleven."

59

The Seeschloss Hotel was a sad seventies building in a breathtaking location—if the postcards displayed at the reception desk were to be believed. It was at the far end of a promontory overgrown with reeds, surrounded by water on three sides, with a view of the distant shores of the neighboring country and the brightly flagged ships on Lake Constance.

Herr Arnold had told his wife he would be away for the night. She was used to all sorts of things. He joined Allmen and Carlos for supper in the almost empty restaurant.

Dinner—oily whitefish in too much batter—passed with sparse conversation. Allmen and Carlos couldn't talk about the burning subject of the day's events in Herr Arnold's presence, so they were restricted to small talk and predicting what the weather would do next.

They went to bed early and arranged to meet for breakfast at ten. This was altered to nine-fifteen after consultation with the waitress. Breakfast was only served till nine-thirty at the Seeschloss.

Once Allmen was alone in his "suite," a slightly larger room with a sofa, chairs and stained wall-to-wall carpeting, he suddenly felt as worn-out as he had after a rugby game thirty years ago at Charterhouse in Surrey.

He slept deeply, without dreams or worries, till his travel alarm woke him again. It was eight o'clock. It had stopped snowing and the thick clouds had become lighter, soon to disperse.

60

There was a smell of overheated drip coffee, evaporating on the burner. In the dining room three solitary businessmen were finishing their breakfast, each at a separate table. The sliced meats and cheeses on the buffet looked as if they had been there all night.

Allmen, Carlos and Herr Arnold sat at one of the many free tables by a window, drank coffee, ate dry rolls with butter and jam from tiny sachets and looked out at the water and the sky, becoming bluer by the minute. They did not say much.

Shortly after ten, Herr Arnold left. They had agreed that he could go for a drive around the area till Allmen called and asked him to return to the Seeschloss. As long as he didn't go too far away.

Allmen and Carlos finished their breakfast and arranged to meet, at ten to eleven at the reception. There was a lounge area where Allmen would wait for Terry. Carlos was to stay somewhere within sight, wearing an earpiece just like a bodyguard.

At a quarter to eleven, Allmen paid the bill for the three rooms, but obtained permission to use his suite a little longer for a short meeting, a request made more emphatic by an ample tip.

Then he sat down in one of the armchairs and waited. Carlos stood a few feet behind him, alert.

One of the businessmen checked out but left his luggage. The other checked out and set off. The third handed in his keys and said, "See you later."

Terry Werenbusch was delayed.

A man who looked as if he had a long drive behind him arrived and double-checked that his room was a no-smoking room.

A couple with a substantial age difference checked in without luggage.

The participants for an event in one of the two seminar rooms started trickling in.

Finally Terry Werenbusch arrived. He was pulling a large wheeled suitcase. He saw Allmen immediately.

Allmen stood up, greeted him from a distance and joined him in the elevator. Carlos followed them.

61

Terry Werenbusch made a strange picture as he unpacked the bowls from the Bubble Wrap. Shy, almost reverent, he held the artworks in his hands with a slightly lowered jaw. He took each one to the window, examining it in the bright daylight, absorbed and oblivious, taking no notice of Allmen and Carlos.

Only as he started to pack the bowls in the tissue and padding he had taken from his suitcase, did Allmen remind him of his presence.

Terry looked up in surprise, remembered where he was and threw a thick yellow envelope onto the bed. According to Carlos—Allmen didn't condescend to count them—it contained exactly five hundred one-thousand notes.

They returned to the lobby like hotel guests who had met for the first time in the elevator, and went their separate ways without a farewell, without turning to look back even once.

62

The return journey passed without incident. The sky was clear now, the temperatures safely back above freezing, the roads clear of snow and Herr Arnold no longer dependent on the traffic news. Glenn Miller was playing again.

Allmen asked Herr Arnold to stop outside the Confédération and wait till he had checked out.

While Carlos packed his things, Allmen called the St. Gallen police force and gave them some extremely valuable information.

63

The sudden warmth had melted most of the snow on the grounds of the Villa Schwarzacker except for a few grayish lumps. After the previous cold weather the leaves had started to drop. The warm foehn wind was ripping them from the branches and creating mischief. Carlos was busy the whole day trying to keep the pathways clear. The manager of the trust company had already reprimanded him repeatedly for choosing to take a day off when it was snowing.

Allmen was restless. But he could hardly call the police and ask how it was going. He had to wait till they called him, which the officer on the telephone had promised to do. "To clear up any further questions," as he had put it.

He would have loved to distract himself with piano playing, and missed his Bechstein. One of the first things he intended to buy was a replacement.

He tried to steer his thoughts elsewhere with the help of Inspector Maigret, which usually did the trick. But the criminal story line reminded him too much of his own situation.

He put the book aside, went to the bookcase and took down one of his other aides in fleeing reality: William Somerset Maugham. It was a book of short stories in English and he read "The Back of Beyond." But even George Moon, the outgoing resident of Timbang Belud, didn't grip him as usual. He stood at the glass wall facing the rear of the garden and stared into the dark green undergrowth through which Terry Werenbusch had shot him.

Carlos had repaired the bullet hole with tape. When Allmen stood in front of it, as now, it was exactly at the height of his heart, which was beating in a frenzy at the thought of how close he had come to death, and how calmly he had dealt with the person who had almost murdered him.

He put a CD on, Neil Young's *Harvest*. But the album reminded him of his time at Charterhouse and thus of Terry. He pressed stop.

Shortly before five he couldn't take it any longer. He got changed, called Herr Arnold and had him drive him to the Golden Bar. There he drank a margarita and tried not to overhear Kellermann, Kunz and Biondi's conversation about Tanner's murder. There were no developments, he gathered. The police still had no clues. But they always said that.

He went without the second margarita, signed the check as usual, although his pockets were stuffed with cash, and headed to Promenade for an early supper.

He browsed the menu of game specials idly but put it aside. He'd had enough of hunters for now. He decided on fish. Something light which wouldn't keep him awake tonight.

Just before ten he went for a nightcap beer back in the Golden Bar, pleasantly quiet at this time. He was in bed before eleven. He read a few pages, switched off the light and let the foehn lull him to sleep.

64

When Allmen woke the pale strip of light on the ceiling above the curtain rod hadn't yet appeared. His alarm said just after five-thirty, far too early for his early morning tea. But he got up. He had to find out if the media had anything new to report on the case of the dragonfly bowls.

He put his dressing gown on and left the bedroom. There was a smell of coffee and toast, untypical at this time. Carlos wished him *"Muy buenos días, Don John,"* and invited him to take a seat in the "salon," as he called it.

There the table was set for breakfast. Next to the plate were computer printouts. Carlos had searched the online press and printed out everything of interest. Here it was at last, the certainty Allmen had been waiting so desperately for.

There had been an unexpected development in an art theft case which had caused a sensation nearly ten years ago; in an exhibition of works by Emile Gallé in St. Gallen, objects valued at several million francs had been stolen, several others destroyed or damaged. A prime suspect had been arrested and the five works, the famous dragonfly bowls, had been secured.

The five! Terry hadn't even managed to hide the four others!

Allmen jumped up, leaped on the bewildered Carlos, who was watching Allmen's reaction from the door, hugged him and kissed him on both cheeks.

Carlos wiped his face in embarrassment. "*Hay más*— there's more." He pointed to the printouts on the table.

The other article was an announcement in the business section. A spokesperson for Hirt Holdings yesterday confirmed that their CEO and sole shareholder Klaus Hirt had died of a heart attack. An obituary would follow.

65

It was now spring. Every deciduous tree on the grounds of the Villa Schwarzacker was a delicate green. The forsythias were singing their yellow into the pale blue sky, while the lilacs hid their purple quietly among their branches.

It was Sunday, the shoe-shine ritual. Allmen was sitting on the raised piano stool next to his new Bechstein, one foot on the black shoe-shine box, watching Carlos, still fascinated by his elegance and dexterity after all these years.

The case of the dragonfly bowls had caused a sensation. More and more details had gradually been made public:

The Werenbusch family, part of the Swiss upper crust, had been in severe financial straits which they navigated by committing insurance fraud. They owned one of the most internationally significant Gallé collections, including the famous dragonfly bowls valued at several million francs. Terry Werenbusch, one of the sons, stole them while they were on loan to the Langturm Museum. With the insurance payout they got out of their tight squeeze and back on their feet.

The matter came to light after nearly ten years when a visitor recognized one of the bowls in a vitrine in the living room of the aging head of the family and informed the police.

A house search at the family seat turned up the four other dragonflies. Forensic evidence gathered in the museum at the time of the robbery now implicated Terry Werenbusch so heavily he had been in custody ever since. Now he would remain in prison until the trial, as a pistol in his possession was identified without doubt as the weapon used in the recent murder of art and antiques dealer Jack Tanner. The police were working on the assumption he was party to information related to the fraud.

Allmen received the reward. Well earned, he felt, considering the police were also able to solve Tanner's murder thanks to an informative tip provided by none other than himself.

A total of nine hundred thousand francs might have seemed a large sum at first. But after handing a hundred thousand to Carlos—this was the agreed fee for his help and for his idea of raising Terry's private reward from four hundred to five hundred—and the acquisition of a new baby grand, there was only around six hundred and sixty thousand left.

Allmen hadn't noticed Carlos's tap on the tip of his sole, the prompt for him to switch feet. The man who was probably the only practicing Guatemalan shoe polisher with a hundred thousand Swiss francs in the bank repeated his signal with barely concealed impatience. Such inattentiveness on the part of his customers broke his rhythm and cost him valuable seconds.

Various urgent repairs and improvements to the gardener's cottage and the library also ate away at the capital. Nor was the repurchase of various rashly sold showpieces from his Art Nouveau furniture collection cheap.

Alongside that he brought all his debts back to tabula rasa. He cleared all his outstanding payments, even to the creditors who had long since given up. This didn't just give him a good feeling. It was also a shrewd way of readjusting his image. He was sure the effect would last, even in times—hopefully not to return—when he might need to rely on it.

In addition, having suffered so long from being tied down, he had undertaken the occasional trip, refreshing his relationships with his Italian and English tailors, and taking the opportunity to have his shoemaker make the repairs to his right upper necessitated by the brutality of the unspeakable Dörig.

This had all reduced him to a balance of somewhere over a hundred thousand francs, which might have lasted him a good while, if he hadn't felt homesick for Aspen. As the date of the festival approached, the feeling grew stronger. And one night he had gone for a nightcap in the Blauer Heinrich after the Golden Bar, then at two in the morning—in Colorado it was only six p.m.—he called The Little Nell, where he had spent some great Christmases, and asked to speak to the manager. He still remembered Allmen, and as luck would have it, a suite had just become free after a regular guest had canceled at short notice. It wasn't one of the very big ones, just a normal executive suite, just right for Allmen and Olivia Goodman ("I absolutely adore European aristocrats") whom he met on his second day there.

This trip to Aspen was the only thing since the dragonfly episode that he placed in the category of "escapades." He had enjoyed it and at no point regretted it, but financially it unfortunately brought him close to the situation he had found himself in before. The only difference was that he had no debts anymore and his creditworthiness was now impeccable. Nevertheless he had recently caught himself dwelling on the subject of potential sources of income. Perhaps even a regular source.

Carlos had just requested he exchange another pair of glossy, polished shoes for an unpolished pair, when he had the idea. "Carlos?"

He didn't look up. *"Qué manda, Don John?"*

"I was just thinking that there are various things for whose recovery rewards are offered."

"Cómo no, Don John."

"Do you think there are people who make a career out of this?"

"Cómo no, there are bounty hunters, after all, Don John."

"True. So what do they call themselves? Reward hunters? Professional advisors? Recoverers?"

"No tengo idea, Don John."

"Rewardeers? Rewarders? *Rewardeurs?"*

Allmen pictured his business card. "Johann Friedrich von Allmen." Times New Roman, 12 point, small caps. Two points smaller, below: "International Enquiries." Looked good.

Carlos tapped the tip of his sole. Allmen swapped feet. An experienced team.

"Carlos?"

"Qué manda, Don John?"

"Do you think that might be a job for us?"

Now Carlos looked up from his work for the first time. He thought briefly and shrugged his shoulders.

"Cómo no, Don John."

AFTERWORD

The five Gallé bowls with the dragonfly motifs were indeed stolen from an exhibition in a burglary at Château de Gingins on October 27, 2004. Investigations continue and the Vaud police are not currently releasing information on their progress.

All other details of this story are invented, and any resemblance to real events is purely coincidental. This applies equally to all places, names and persons appearing in the novel.

Martin Suter

THE LAST WEYNFELDT
BY MARTIN SUTER

Adrian Weynfeldt is an art expert in an international auction house, a bachelor in his mid-fifties living in a grand Zurich apartment filled with costly paintings and antiques. Always correct and well-mannered, he's given up on love until one night—entirely out of character for him—Weynfeldt decides to take home a ravishing but unaccountable young woman and gets embroiled in an art forgery scheme that threatens his buttoned up existence. This refined page-turner moves behind elegant bourgeois facades into darker recesses of the heart.

THE MADELEINE PROJECT
BY CLARA BEAUDOUX

A young woman moves into a Paris apartment and discovers a storage room filled with the belongings of the previous owner, a certain Madeleine who died in her late nineties, and whose treasured possessions nobody seems to want. In an audacious act of journalism driven by personal curiosity and humane tenderness, Clara Beaudoux embarks on *The Madeleine Project*, documenting what she finds on Twitter with text and photographs, introducing the world to an unsung 20th century figure.

A VERY FRENCH CHRISTMAS

A continuation of the very popular Very Christmas Series, this collection brings together the best French Christmas stories of all time in an elegant and vibrant collection featuring classics by Guy de Maupassant and Alphonse Daudet, plus stories by the esteemed twentieth century author Irène Némirovsky and contemporary writers Dominique Fabre and Jean-Philippe Blondel. With a holiday spirit conveyed through sparkling Paris streets, opulent feasts, wandering orphans, flickering desire, and more than a little wine, this collection proves that the French have mastered Christmas.

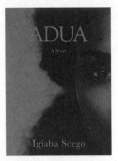

ADUA BY IGIABA SCEGO

Adua, an immigrant from Somalia to Italy, has lived in Rome for nearly forty years. She came seeking freedom from a strict father and an oppressive regime, but her dreams of film stardom ended in shame. Now that the civil war in Somalia is over, her homeland calls her. She must decide whether to return and reclaim her inheritance, but also how to take charge of her own story and build a future.

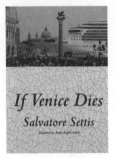

IF VENICE DIES BY SALVATORE SETTIS

Internationally renowned art historian Salvatore Settis ignites a new debate about the Pearl of the Adriatic and cultural patrimony at large. In this fiery blend of history and cultural analysis, Settis argues that "hit-and-run" visitors are turning Venice and other landmark urban settings into shopping malls and theme parks. This is a passionate plea to secure the soul of Venice, written with consummate authority, wide-ranging erudition and élan.

A VERY RUSSIAN CHRISTMAS

This is Russian Christmas celebrated in supreme pleasure and pain by the greatest of writers, from Dostoevsky and Tolstoy to Chekhov and Teffi. The dozen stories in this collection will satisfy every reader, and with their wit, humor, and tenderness, packed full of sentimental songs, footmen, whirling winds, solitary nights, snow drifts, and hopeful children, the collection proves that Nobody Does Christmas Like the Russians.

THE MADONNA OF NOTRE DAME
BY ALEXIS RAGOUGNEAU

Fifty thousand people jam into Notre Dame Cathedral to celebrate the Feast of the Assumption. The next morning, a beautiful young woman clothed in white kneels at prayer in a cathedral side chapel. But when someone accidentally bumps against her, her body collapses. She has been murdered. This thrilling novel illuminates shadowy corners of the world's most famous cathedral, shedding light on good and evil with suspense, compassion and wry humor.

THE YEAR OF THE COMET
BY SERGEI LEBEDEV

A story of a Russian boyhood and coming of age as the Soviet Union is on the brink of collapse. Lebedev depicts a vast empire coming apart at the seams, transforming a very public moment into something tender and personal, and writes with stunning beauty and shattering insight about childhood and the growing consciousness of a boy in the world.

MOVING THE PALACE
BY CHARIF MAJDALANI

A young Lebanese adventurer explores the wilds of Africa, encountering an eccentric English colonel in Sudan and enlisting in his service. In this lush chronicle of far-flung adventure, the military recruit crosses paths with a compatriot who has dismantled a sumptuous palace and is transporting it across the continent on a camel caravan. This is a captivating modern-day Odyssey in the tradition of Bruce Chatwin and Paul Theroux.

THE 6:41 TO PARIS
BY JEAN-PHILIPPE BLONDEL

Cécile, a stylish 47-year-old, has spent the weekend visiting her parents outside Paris. By Monday morning, she's exhausted. These trips back home are stressful and she settles into a train compartment with an empty seat beside her. But it's soon occupied by a man she recognizes as Philippe Leduc, with whom she had a passionate affair that ended in her brutal humiliation 30 years ago. In the fraught hour and a half that ensues, Cécile and Philippe hurtle towards the French capital in a psychological thriller about the pain and promise of past romance.

ON THE RUN WITH MARY
BY JONATHAN BARROW

Shining moments of tender beauty punctuate this story of a youth on the run after escaping from an elite English boarding school. At London's Euston Station, the narrator meets a talking dachshund named Mary and together they're off on escapades through posh Mayfair streets and jaunts in a Rolls-Royce. But the youth soon realizes that the seemingly sweet dog is a handful; an alcoholic, nymphomaniac, drug-addicted mess who can't stay out of pubs or off the dance floor. *On the Run with Mary* mirrors the horrors and the joys of the terrible 20th century.

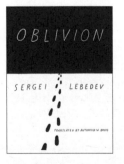

OBLIVION BY SERGEI LEBEDEV

In one of the first 21st century Russian novels to probe the legacy of the Soviet prison camp system, a young man travels to the vast wastelands of the Far North to uncover the truth about a shadowy neighbor who saved his life, and whom he knows only as Grandfather II. Emerging from today's Russia, where the ills of the past are being forcefully erased from public memory, this masterful novel represents an epic literary attempt to rescue history from the brink of oblivion.

THE LAST SUPPER BY KLAUS WIVEL

Alarmed by the oppression of 7.5 million Christians in the Middle East, journalist Klaus Wivel traveled to Iraq, Lebanon, Egypt, and the Palestinian territories to learn about their fate. He found a minority under threat of death and humiliation, desperate in the face of rising Islamic extremism and without hope their situation will improve. An unsettling account of a severely beleaguered religious group living, so it seems, on borrowed time. Wivel asks, Why have we not done more to protect these people?

GUYS LIKE ME BY DOMINIQUE FABRE

Dominique Fabre, born in Paris and a life-long resident of the city, exposes the shadowy, anonymous lives of many who inhabit the French capital. In this quiet, subdued tale, a middle-aged office worker, divorced and alienated from his only son, meets up with two childhood friends who are similarly adrift. He's looking for a second act to his mournful life, seeking the harbor of love and a true connection with his son. Set in palpably real Paris streets that feel miles away from the City of Light, a stirring novel of regret and absence, yet not without a glimmer of hope.

ANIMAL INTERNET BY ALEXANDER PSCHERA

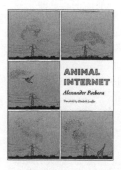

Some 50,000 creatures around the globe—including whales, leopards, flamingoes, bats and snails—are being equipped with digital tracking devices. The data gathered and studied by major scientific institutes about their behavior will warn us about tsunamis, earthquakes and volcanic eruptions, but also radically transform our relationship to the natural world. Contrary to pessimistic fears, author Alexander Pschera sees the Internet as creating a historic opportunity for a new dialogue between man and nature.

KILLING AUNTIE BY **ANDRZEJ BURSA**

A young university student named Jurek, with no particular ambitions or talents, finds himself with nothing to do. After his doting aunt asks the young man to perform a small chore, he decides to kill her for no good reason other than, perhaps, boredom. This short comedic masterpiece combines elements of Dostoevsky, Sartre, Kafka, and Heller, coming together to produce an unforgettable tale of murder and—just maybe—redemption.

I CALLED HIM NECKTIE BY **MILENA MICHIKO FLAŠAR**

Twenty-year-old Taguchi Hiro has spent the last two years of his life living as a hikikomori—a shut-in who never leaves his room and has no human interaction—in his parents' home in Tokyo. As Hiro tentatively decides to reenter the world, he spends his days observing life from a park bench. Gradually he makes friends with Ohara Tetsu, a salaryman who has lost his job. The two discover in their sadness a common bond. This beautiful novel is moving, unforgettable, and full of surprises.

WHO IS MARTHA? BY **MARJANA GAPONENKO**

In this rollicking novel, 96-year-old ornithologist Luka Levadski foregoes treatment for lung cancer and moves from Ukraine to Vienna to make a grand exit in a luxury suite at the Hotel Imperial. He reflects on his past while indulging in Viennese cakes and savoring music in a gilded concert hall. Levadski was born in 1914, the same year that Martha—the last of the now-extinct passenger pigeons—died. Levadski himself has an acute sense of being the last of a species. This gloriously written tale mixes piquant wit with lofty musings about life, friendship, aging and death.

![New Vessel Press logo] New Vessel Press

*To purchase these books and for a full listing
of New Vessel Press titles, visit our website at
www.newvesselpress.com*